Island of the Super People

Dedicated to the super people of the world.

Also to the specific super people who helped me write this book in fantastic ways—the Eraserhead Press crew and my family. Thank you all for your patience and for helping me realize my powers.

ISLAND OF THE SUPER PEOPLE

KEVIN SHAMEL

ERASERHEAD PRESS
PORTLAND, OREGON

ERASERHEAD PRESS
205 NE BRYANT
PORTLAND, OR 97211

WWW.ERASERHEADPRESS.COM

ISBN: 1-936383-81-0

Author's Note

This is a very special book for me. The process of its creation signifies my journey as a writer.

Island of the Super People was written during the first ever Bizarro Bootcamp, in June of 2010. I was a New Bizarro Author at the time. Bootcamp was a full-on hardcore introduction into professional authoring. Led by Carlton Mellick III and Rose O'Keefe, the instructors included polished pros Cameron Pierce, Jeff Burk, Mykle Hansen, and Jeremy Robert Johnson. It was an immersion into the bizarro scene and the business of publishing as well as instruction on how to write quality fiction. And a shitload of fun.

I wrote the first draft in five days. Trial by fire. I came out of bootcamp with a book written and the skills to write more.

I write this note having just finished the layout for this book. It's the first one I've ever done. My journey has taken me even farther into the bizarro world. I'm now an editor at Eraserhead Press, for the New Bizarro Author Series. And I lay-out books now, as well as bring new authors to you. It's been quite a year.

This is more than just a book to me. It's a representation of a very special year in my life as a writer. And I think it's SUPER.

I hope you enjoy the story.

Chapter One

A large, muscular man surfaced near the bow of the ship, bounding through the water like a dolphin. His scaly green skin glittered in the sunlight. Octopus suckers decorated the backs of his arms and legs. He looked up at the ship through tendrils of seaweed colored hair and winked an ocean-blue eye.

Professor Topper leaned against the rail, pointing at the surface of the water. He explained to a group of interns what they were witnessing. "Take a good look at your first super sapien, students. That's Whalemancer—the super man of the sea."

"So he's a seaman?" Martin said, pronouncing it, *semen*. He chuckled and raised his hand to Trent for a high-five. Trent ignored him.

Jen opened her notebook. "What are Whalemancer's powers?"

"He can telepathically speak to whales and breathe underwater. He lives in the ocean most of the time. He usually sleeps while he swims, like a shark."

"He sleeps with sharks?" Martin asked quietly. He looked to Trent, but was ignored.

"Does he have webbed hands and feet?" Jen asked, scratching down notes.

"Yes, he does indeed have webbing. He has gills as well, and when his ankles are aligned, they resemble a caudle fin—a tailfin." The professor continued his lecture on the aquatic superhero.

Trent hung back from the group, trying not to puke. He'd

been seasick ever since they left port for the Island of the Super People. He wondered again if he should even be there.

Unlike Jen, he wasn't the brightest of Professor's Topper's students. He didn't have rich parents to put money toward the trip like Martin. He was just an average student going for his master's degree in Cultural Anthropology. But he was about to spend the next three months on a very special expedition, studying a tribe of super-powered primitives. Living on a tropical island in the Pacific Ocean—a chance of a lifetime. Trent wasn't really sure why he'd been chosen to go. He flipped open his notebook to sketch Whalemancer. He wanted to get down details, like the suckers.

"Mr. Derring, do you have any observations about Whalemancer you'd like to share?" Professor Topper smiled at Trent, as if Topper knew he hadn't been paying attention.

"Uh. Well, he seems to have a great rate of propulsion. Is his musculature shark-like, as well?" Trent burped silently. Vomit stung the back of his throat. He sketched, craning to see the super man.

The professor's smile widened. "Actually, it's more like a squid. But I like how you're thinking."

Trent nodded and returned a slight smile. His stomach lurched.

Natalie, the professor's assistant, came above-deck. She was writing on a clipboard. Her thick-framed glasses slid down her nose as she inspected crates of their equipment. She pushed the glasses up and turned to the students. "We've just left cell phone range. If you needed to make a last call before reaching the island, it's too late."

"What the hell?" Martin said. "Why didn't you tell me sooner?"

Natalie ignored his comment and returned to her clipboard, her glasses slipping down her nose again.

Whalemancer leapt out of the water, splashing Jen with water. She frowned at the Professor, her notebook and blouse soaked. He just smiled at her and gave her a pat on the back. The super man of the sea dove out of sight.

"Just an hour or so and we'll be among the super people,"

the Professor said, staring off at the speck of land in the distance.

"Among the hot super chicks," Martin said. He looked at Trent with a big dumb smile.

Trent went back to sketching.

Chapter Two

The dock looked rotted. There were obviously loose boards, and most were warped. The wood was grey and stained with salt. If several crewmembers hadn't already started unloading their supplies, Trent would have expected to fall through the rickety thing.

The captain met with them about the boat's scheduled return at the end of the season. Natalie went over the manifest as supplies were unloaded. Professor Topper practically ran down the gangplank once he was free to leave. The students followed their professor along the rickety, decrepit dock, stepping gingerly to avoid the worst looking boards.

Two super people came walking out of the forest to greet them.

"Oh my God, get a look at those tits!" Martin poked Trent in the ribs.

Trent ignored Martin. But he did get a look at the physiques of the super sapiens. It was impossible not to notice the bulging muscles of the male, and the cartoonishly large breasts of the female. The man's chest was as impressive. Beyond that, the rest of their bodies were over-inflated. Their red, white, and blue suits were filled out in cartoonish proportion. Their muscles bulged. They were beautiful and odd, with chiseled features and perfect hair. Like characters in a comic book come to life. It was hard to believe they were real. *Super* was a perfect word to describe them.

The woman's suit was a white, low-cut leotard with blue stars across it. She had a red headband. The man wore a blue bodysuit with a lightning bolt across the chest. A red hood masked his face from the nose up. The super woman was blonde, with blue eyes and Miss Universe teeth. The man had perfect posture and a blinding smile.

Jen pulled out her notebook and began scribbling.

"Oh, look!" the professor said to his students. "It's Heat Vixen and Lightning Ray!" He skipped down the dock ahead of the students.

The woman smiled at Professor Topper as she approached. She opened her mouth as if to speak to the professor. But instead of a voice, a small white bubble oozed out of her mouth. It floated out of her lips and expanded like a balloon. When it was inflated, it was a large white oval hovering above her head, connected to her mouth by a thin, pointy tail.

Black text formed on the front of the bubble. The words read: *Greetings, Topper*!

Trent marveled at witnessing his first speech bubble— the super people's way of communicating. They do not have developed voices, or understand any form of verbal language. All three of the students knew this about the super sapiens, but were amazed to see it in person. The bubbles were as white as paper, yet had a moist gummy texture to them, as if organic.

The speech bubble swayed gently above the woman's head as the professor read it. Then the bubble dissolved. Its edges faded, and it popped and was gone.

When the super man blew a bubble to speak, the text inside read, *Topper! It's been many seasons!*

Jen gaped at the man's bubble, madly scribbling. She searched around after it popped, looking for remnants. There were none.

The professor pulled a white balloon and black marker from his pocket. He blew up the balloon. There was a squeaking noise as he wrote on the balloon with the marker. Then he held up the makeshift speech bubble to the side of his head.

The balloon read, *It's great to be back!*

The islanders spoke again, but Trent missed what was written on their speech bubbles. Having difficulty reading the dialogue bubbles from his distance, he looked away from their conversation. Natalie arrived beside him carrying a cardboard box. She handed him a large baggie filled with balloons and two black markers.

"You each get a supply of one hundred balloons for communicating with the natives," she told the students, as she passed baggies to Jen and Martin, "use them wisely."

Trent zipped his speaking supplies in his backpack. When he stood up, Martin was already writing text on an inflated balloon. Trent wondered who he was planning on communicating with until he saw what he had written.

The frat boy lifted the balloon up to his head, as if speaking to Trent. Thick block letters spelled out, *BOOBS!* Martin pointed at the busty super woman and raised his eyebrows. Trent frowned and moved away. Martin continued holding the word balloon to his head and followed after him.

When the super duo finished their conversation with the professor, they turned and walked off toward a path leading into the jungle and waited for the group.

Professor Topper hefted his pack and turned to his students. "Let's go! Heat Vixen and Lightning Ray will take us to their village." He said to his assistant, "Nat, you stay here and organize the equipment. We'll be back soon."

They followed the super people into the jungle.

Trent brought up the rear behind Martin, who still held his word balloon over his head. His mouth gaped open. He stared at the super woman's curvy white butt. Martin noticed that Trent saw him drooling over the woman's excessively round ass, gave Trent a thumbs-up, and went back to gawking.

Jen took notes, devouring the super people with her eyes and paying little attention to where she was going. The professor walked in front of her, beside the two super people, speaking with them. The students could see their speech bubbles, but being behind them, they couldn't read what was said.

The group came out of the trees into a wide, grassy clearing.

Dozens of super people surrounded them.

They flew through the sky, tunneled through the earth, shot ice balls at one another in some sort of game, jumped through rings of fire, and ran blurry-fast against each other in sprints and dashes. The wide field was filled with activity.

The vivid color of the super people in their red, white, and blue suits clashed against drab straw huts lining the dirt path through the super people's village.

Trent stopped and stared. Speech bubbles inflated and popped all around. Fires leapt from spaces between huts. A woman seemingly made of water ran past, splashing across the path and leaving muddy tracks.

Jen stopped taking notes. She became so distracted by the fliers in the air, fire, lightning bolts, and exploding speech bubbles that she bumped into the professor. Martin finally deflated his balloon and was staring at the super women that flew past or sat at fire pits in front of their huts.

Several super people gathered in a large open space around a wide stone well in the village square. There was a woman with blue skin and hair. Her costume was a white and blue polka-dotted bikini and a red mask over her eyes. She jumped high into the sky as a woman in a blue skirt, white bikini-top with two red stars over her nipples, and high red boots tried to catch her with a lasso. Super children scampered around, playing tag by teleporting and turning invisible.

A man near the center of the village stretched his body so that his head was above the trees. He swung his red-hooded head on a long, loopy neck. He smiled at them as he whipped past.

The professor came to a halt near a big tree before the group was too near the huts. He said, "Welcome to Hero Village." He smiled at the shaken students. "I know it's overwhelming. That's why I want you to spend some time right here—to get a feel for the place. You basically know what to expect, and you know the protocols of how to behave.

"Remember that we observe politely. We will usually keep our distance. There are some super people like Lightning Ray and Heat Vixen that may be friendly, but for the most part do not push it. After we've observed for a moment, I'm going to give you each a chance to introduce yourself to a villager. The people here are fairly used to anthropologists, but most will ignore us unless we open a dialogue."

The students watched the villagers. They seemed to be either entertaining themselves and others with their powers, cooking, or conversing with each other. Obviously, a typical day in the village.

Each person's super suit was different, though they were all red, white, and blue. Nearly every super person was muscular, and the ones who weren't seemed to be designed that way on purpose—like the stretchy ones, or the ones shaped like animals or objects.

The students stood and watched.

After ten minutes, the professor told his students to go forward, find one super person, and introduce themselves.

"You'll be fine," he told them. "Don't be long, and come right back here."

Trent didn't think he'd be fine. He figured he'd most likely offend someone. But he blew up a balloon, wrote, *Hi, I'm Trent.* on it, and held it over his head as he walked down the path.

Jen scampered ahead of the others, heading straight for a super man and woman who sat in hammocks outside a hut, nibbling on big pink fruits. She paused to pop Martin's re-inflated *BOOBS!* balloon with her pen before he got himself killed. Jen's own balloon introduced her, and the man and woman seemed friendly when she approached, even offering her a fruit. She accepted, but graciously departed soon after.

Martin didn't bother to blow up a new balloon. He headed for a hut where three super women sat around a fire, roasting birds. He stood near them for a while. He didn't last long under the super women's stares.

Trent found a super man sculpting with fire. The man stood in an open area and added flames from his hands to a tall spinning seahorse made of fire. As he pushed more flames into the sculpture, it flared orange-white and smoke billowed from the animal's nose.

While the sculptor was busy at work, Trent examined his suit. It was blue and white striped—a typical one-piece looking outfit like you'd find in any comic book. There was a large red star on his chest, with a white flame in its center. He had a red cape and a blue mask.

Super people suits are not clothing. They are a part of their skin. Each super person is born in his or her costume and it develops as they grow. The cape on the super man's back wasn't a cape, but a sheet of blue flesh. His mask was puffed-up cheekbones and an inflated brow.

Trent could see nerves and tendons within the super man's cape. It was more like the wing of a bat. The blue and white stripes on the man's body were skin coloring. The red star on his chest was a birthmark. His nipples showed underneath.

What looked like red boots were just raised flesh and melted-together toes. As the super man moved around, Trent could see that they were just as much a part of his legs as his knees. Around the sculptor's pelvis the suit was raised, like he wore a different colored swimsuit. His dick was definitely exposed, but colored so that from a distance he didn't look naked at all.

Weird. Trent reached out to touch the man's cape and thought better of it.

When the super man glanced over at him, Trent held up his balloon. The man frowned at him and went back to work. Trent looked at his balloon and realized he was holding it backward. He flipped the balloon around and held it up beside his mouth.

When the fire-sculptor looked back and didn't acknowledge his greeting, Trent thought the balloon might not be blown up enough. As the super man looked on, Trent over-inflated his balloon and it popped.

A speech bubble shot out of the super man's mouth. It was jagged and pointy, not at all like the soft ones with rounded edges that Trent had seen so far. Trent recognized it from his studies as the type of bubble used for exclamations. Trent read, *Get out of here!*

He did. He joined the rest of the group gathered at the big tree.

"How did you do, Trent?" the professor asked as he arrived.

Trent said, "Uh. I did fine. Saw a fire sculptor."

Jen started talking about how great her experience was. Trent ignored her and watched people flying around. Martin was quiet and had a dazed sort of look about him.

"Well, let's head back to the dock, gather our supplies, and set up camp," the professor said. He motioned for them to follow the trail.

On the way, the professor said, "Heat Vixen and Lightning Ray told me about a special ceremonial feast tonight. We are going to observe it. It's a rare thing for an anthropologist to witness. We should consider ourselves very lucky. Heat Vixen told me it would be okay for us to attend, but we will have to keep a low profile. It's very exciting!"

Jen asked, "What kind of ceremony? A naming ceremony? Manhood rites? Womanhood?"

"Be patient, Jennifer. I don't know. We'll all find out tonight," the professor told her.

They soon arrived at their pile of supplies.

Natalie was there, going through their equipment, reading the manifest. The ship was gone.

"Nat, if you could…" Professor Topper let the rest of the sentence hang and stared over the top of his assistant's head. "Oh my," he said.

The students followed his gaze. The professor had discovered Whalemancer standing on the beach.

"Natalie, how long has he been there?"

"Who?" Natalie pushed her glasses up.

Dr. Topper dismissed her with a wave. "Follow me, students."

He hurried down the beach toward the oceanic super man.

Jen stopped to grab her video camera.

Trent and Martin lagged behind. Trent was a little frightened of Whalemancer—he had an aversion to suckers and seafood. Martin wasn't all that interested in a fish dude.

Professor Topper gathered his students fifty feet from the super man. He told them, "As I said, Whalemancer rarely comes out of the water. There must be something going on."

Trent noticed a shimmering around the super man's head, like heat waves.

Jen looked up from the camera's viewfinder and asked, "Does Whalemancer have a telepathic connection with animals other than whales?"

"Shh, Jennifer. No. Observe." The professor pointed.

The shimmering around Whalemancer's head intensified. Glowing circles of telepathic energy rippled from his head toward the ocean like smoke rings. The surface of the water foamed. The super man's circular telepathy glowed brighter. A spout of water shot into the air, and a huge gray-blue head broke through the crashing waves.

A whale flopped itself onto the beach, its tail curling high above the rolling waves breaking around its giant body.

Whalemancer stood with his arms stretched outward. The spheres of mental energy coming from his head beamed straight at the whale's. The cetacean's massive eyes rolled up in their sockets. The creature screeched. The sea man beamed hard circles at the whale. Rings of energy penetrated the whale's head. Trent wondered what it would be like to bend to Whalemancer's will.

The whale gathered itself in the pounding surf and wormed its way further onto the sand. A huge plume of beach grit showered the anthropologists. They turned and ran.

"What's happening?" Jen shouted, stopping behind Professor Topper.

"Whalemancer is feeding the village!" the professor yelled.

The students re-gathered.

Whalemancer strode toward the whale, his thought-beams burning the air around him, piercing the giant's skull. Trent could almost smell the whale's brain being singed with plasmic thoughts from the sea man. The super man maneuvered the whale further onto the beach. Only the creature's tail was left in the lapping waves. One final spastic lurch forward and the whale came free of the sea.

"Amazing," Jen said.

"This bounty will feed the village for days," the professor said.

"That's horrible," Trent said. "Isn't it an endangered species?"

Martin scoffed, "Fucking Greenpeacer."

While they gathered supplies, Professor Topper explained further how rare the situation was. He babbled happily about it all the way to their campsite.

Chapter Three

The sun was setting by the time the anthropologists arrived at the village feast. They came upon the dining circle just as the dancers were finishing and the food was being passed around.

Hundreds of super people sat, crouched, stood, and hovered in a tremendous ring of tables and chairs, several layers deep. Red, white, and blue shone in the growing dusk and firelight. Capes fluttered. Speech bubbles expanded and dissipated all around the circle.

The professor led them to a low platform in the middle of the encircled throng. Five super people sat at a long, wide table. He said, "This is the leader. Just stay behind me."

A woman with long white hair sat in an ornate chair at the table's center. She sucked roasted roaches off a stick. Her suit was red, and a dark blue spider stretched across her ample bosom. She had a short white cape with a red hourglass in its center. She wasn't masked.

The professor knelt before her with a balloon and his inflating gun. He put the barrel of the gun to the balloon and pulled the trigger. The balloon filled instantly. The air gun allowed the professor to speak the super person language nearly fluently. Dr. Topper scribbled on the balloon and showed it to his students before holding it up to the super woman. It read, *Madam Manifestor, we are honored to attend this feast.*

The super woman looked down on the anthropologists and scowled. She spoke a long, fat speech bubble, *We didn't know you'd be attending our ceremony. You may sit at the rear table.* She pointed to the outside edge of the circle, at a splintery rectangular table that was sparsely populated. The heroes seated around it were obviously the village rejects.

The professor blew up another balloon with his gun. He told her, *Madame, by your leave, we will join the feast.*

The super woman nodded dismissively.

Professor Topper led the students to the table. He seated each of them away from each other.

Trent sat beside a super person with a fly head. He didn't want to look at the grotesque man for fear of losing what little appetite he had. Trent was nervous about eating the food on the island. He had been a strict vegetarian since his first year in college. He hoped they would be serving vegetables.

Jen settled into relaxed conversation with the super man sitting next to her who seemed to be made of large mossy boulders and clumps of grass.

Martin sat beside a super woman with a hyena head who drooled onto the edge of the table and into her lap. Heat Vixen sat down on the other side of Martin, and Lightning Ray sat beside her next to Jen.

The professor took a chair across the table from Jen beside a very thin super man. The blue and white emblem on his red suit was too skinny to interpret. He had only one eye, one nostril, and one big tooth that stuck out of his tiny, pursed mouth.

Trent noticed a bald boy sitting at the end of the table by himself. Not even the losery heroes paid him any attention. He seemed to be the reject of the rejects.

Jen looked down the table at Trent and Martin. She said, "It's important to eat whatever you're served. It would be extremely rude, maybe even dangerous, to refuse food. I've spent the past nine months preparing for this. I've eaten roaches, worms, pond scum, bark, deer scat, rotten leaves, maggots, carrion… you name it. Just thought I'd remind you boys to eat up."

Martin sighed.

Trent nodded, feeling suddenly sick.

A huge wooden bowl came down the circle. Each person dipped their hand in it and pulled out a dripping white fistful of grayish slurry. A super woman with a lightning bolt on her gigantic breasts passed the bowl to the anthropologists' table.

It came to Trent. He wanted to sniff at it, but knew he couldn't. He shoved his hand into the bowl, closing it around a warm, pulpy, poi-like handful of whatever it was. He passed the bowl to the fly guy. Trent tried to ignore it as the guy puked in his palm and then sucked up the stuff through his straw tongue.

The professor told Trent and Martin, "This is whale blubber soup. It's a delicacy. Lick your hand clean." He turned to Jen.

Trent watched the professor tell Jen what she was going to be eating. Jen's eyes widened. Trent dug at the dirt with his foot, discretely hollowing out a shallow trench while still holding the goo in his palm.

Jen crossed her arms and shook her head. The rocky super person beside her told her something from inside a long, fat speech bubble. She seemed to calm down.

Martin said to Trent, "I hope it's baby whale. They've got the best blubber."

"Shut up, Martin. You know where this came from." Trent deepened the trench in the dirt and casually let the soup drip from his hand. He covered it and wiped his hand on his pants.

The fly guy beside him nudged his shoulder. Trent didn't want to, but he looked over at him. A sour yellow-grayish speech bubble slid from his mouthparts. *Fries!*

The super man handed Trent a stick of skewered, roasted grubs. Trent saw that the man had two in his hand, already dissolving in a puddle of acidic fly vomit.

He passed the stick to a blue-skinned, leathery looking, bat-nosed woman on the other side of him. Her flabby white suit had red and blue smears across it.

Trent watched Jen dip her hand into the bowl when it came to her. He saw the professor watching her as well. Jen pulled out a fistful of the gloppy warm fat and sucked it out of her hand. Trent's stomach flopped for her.

He read some of the conversation between the skinny cyclops and the fat bat woman beside him.

You didn't provoke it?

Who needs to provoke a nemesis? I was just looking for eggs.

Still. He should have given you some warning.

Yeah, even a wicked laugh, or sinister hello. I thought the same thing.

A great, wobbly cube of whale was passed hand-by-hand down the table toward the students. The surface of the oily meat shone orange and yellow under candles and torchlight. People tore chunks or simply took a huge bite off the steaming square of it.

Martin held the gob of whale meat in both his hands, and bit into it with his whole face. The frat boy came away with a mouthful and a glazed cheeks. Thick yellow grease dripped off his chin as he mashed whale between his lips.

"Oh, you're gonna *love* this," he said to Trent. His eyes were wild in the firelight.

Heat Vixen took the hunk of whale from him and held it to her face, tipping her head back to chew. Grease gushed from the cube of meat, splashing onto her breasts and cascading between them. A fat speech bubble slid from her lips. *Mmmmmm!*

Martin howled through his mouthful, spraying gelatinous globs in a chunky mist. He gawked at the super woman's slicked-up, ample chest and Trent rolled his eyes, picturing the frat boy with his friends, getting booted from strip clubs all night long.

Heat Vixen noticed Martin staring. When he finally met her eyes and realized he'd been busted, he winked at her. She went back to ignoring him and passed the meat along.

The chunk of whale came to Trent. He looked to the professor, who nodded.

Trent stared at his teacher. He shook his head slightly. He said, "I can't."

Professor Topper nodded casually, smiling at the heroes around the table, who mostly ignored him. "You have to. It would be extremely bad for all of us if you didn't."

The big batty woman was looking down at the gnawed-on whale cube in Trent's hands.

"Just eat it, you pussy." Martin leaned over the hyena woman's breasts.

"Not eating meat doesn't make me a pussy." Trent started shaking. The whale chunk shimmied in his hands. It looked a little like raw tofu. He thought of that.

"Come, Trent, the rest of the table is waiting," said the professor. "Now."

"You can do it, Trent." Jen said.

Natalie cleared her throat.

Trent looked around and saw that people were beginning to notice. He held his breath, silently asked the animal kingdom to forgive him, and took a tiny bite of whale. It reminded him of tuna he'd eaten before he went vegetarian. He tried to pretend that's what it was. The bat woman snatched the meat from his hands.

As he gagged the bite down, Trent watched two super people near Natalie enjoying their meal together. One of them had metal claws for hands, with long needle fingers. He was stabbing chunks of whale meat and holding them up for the man beside him, who blasted them with fire from his long, tubular anteater nose. Then they each picked the morsels off their kebobs.

Jen looked to Lightning Ray, who nodded sagely. *Big bite.*

She pushed her face into the communal meat cube and came away chewing and smiling. She nodded happily at the heroes around her.

Trent finished his own bite of whale and watched Jen pull out a balloon to talk to her new super friend beside her. Jen's lips were so greasy that when she tried to blow up the balloon, it shot out, farting in crazy circles. When she tried again, the same thing happened. Trent watched her try four times until she embarrassedly gave up.

The mossy super man put his hand on her shoulder and an excited bubble popped out of his shaggy mouth. *You like it so much, you can't speak!*

Jen laughed loudly.

More food was passed in the circle. Trent watched the blue lips of the woman beside him. Red bug flecks covered them, shimmering in the firelight. It looked like she wore purple lip gloss.

She spoke to the fly man. *Are there more fries?*

Drumbeats began. Fires blazed. Super people stood and danced toward the center of the circle. The professor went with Heat Vixen and Lightning Ray into the crowd, toward the central platform. Natalie followed them. Martin ate more. Jen sat at the table, looking in a bit of a daze.

Trent walked toward the outside of the circle. Stars shone in the night sky. Torches and fires lit the village, growing sparser away from the feast. He headed toward the dark shadow of a tree near a cluster of huts.

He leaned against the tree and watched the scene around him. Soon he moved into the firelight on the other side of the tree and pulled out his notebook to sketch the scene at the feast. That's when he heard a baby crying.

Trent turned and saw a woman sitting at a fire, holding a super infant in her arms. He smiled at the baby's little blue tasseled boots and red cape. Its chest symbol was a white triangle with red inside. Most of the skin on its torso was red save for a light ring of lemon yellow surrounding its little stub of umbilical cord and spiraling out across its belly.

The baby's chest emblem seemed to be a wave, or maybe a cloud. Trent knew that when super sapiens are babies, their details aren't well-defined. The colors of their suits are sometimes faded. Their chest symbol might be undeveloped, and may not even become intelligible until puberty.

The super mother rocked her crying baby in her red-gloved arms. Then Trent noticed that the woman was crying, too. Tears dripped down her blue-masked cheek. When she looked up at Trent, he could see a distressed look in her eyes. He wondered what was upsetting her and considered blowing up a question mark balloon but thought better of it.

Behind him, at the circle, the drums stopped.

Trent went back.

Madam Manifestor stood on the platform speaking in fat bubbles.

The super woman spun in a slow circle, and Trent noticed that something was falling around her feet as she did. A gossamer thread waved around her as she turned. It grew and thickened. Trent realized it was thick spider silk when he saw spinnerets working just below her tailbone, pulling thread from her body.

Suddenly the web shot into the air and unfurled like a parachute. It slowly settled down upon the crowd.

Professor Topper left the circle, gathering the students as he went. He led them away from the red, white, and blue crowd and back toward the well in the village square.

They saw the heroes leaving the feast in a wide line, carrying torches into the jungle, their flames flickering between the black trees in the distance.

The professor whispered, "You guys are in for a special treat. I learned from Lightning Ray and Heat Vixen what this feast is about. We're going to see a ceremony that very few outsiders have ever witnessed. Come, back down the path."

They followed the professor into the dark jungle.

Chapter Four

Professor Topper stopped the group just inside the trees. "Turn off your flashlights, everyone. Gather around."

When the students were huddled together, the professor whisper-shouted, "We must hurry along. We must be very quiet, but we're in for a most amazing experience tonight."

Trent immediately felt uneasy.

The professor said, "Come with me. Do not use any lights. Keep silent. We're not invited to this, and I'm not sure what will happen if we are discovered."

Trent's heart quickened.

The group followed their teacher through the blackened jungle.

Martin put himself behind Natalie, in an effort to get as much of a view of her ass as he could in the patchy shadows. Jen followed Martin, and Trent was last in line.

He tapped Jen on the shoulder. "Do you know what's going on?"

"Shh!" she answered.

"Come on, Jen. Do you know where we're going?"

"Be quiet!"

The professor hushed them.

Ten minutes later Trent saw lights flickering. Soon the jungle opened up in front of them into a clearing.

Big lanterns on wooden poles lit the grassy meadow.

Professor Topper took the students to the edge of the trees near one of the lanterns, but kept in the shadows. He whispered, "We'll stay here and observe. Remember, be silent. We don't want to be found out."

Trent squatted beside Jen and looked around. He saw six

lanterns, set in a circle. Some glowed yellow, others white. One was blue.

Martin cleared his throat and spit. "Ugh."

Jen shushed him.

"Shut up. I don't feel so good. I think that whale blubber wasn't cooked or something."

"It's cuz you ate the whole whale," Trent said.

"Shh!" Natalie said. "Be quiet. Stay still."

Everyone was quiet.

Martin moaned.

Trent nudged Jen and whispered, "Do you know what this is?"

"Are you kidding me?"

Trent frowned. "No."

Jen turned and looked at him. Her eyes flashed in the yellow lamplight. "What, are you Martin now?"

Martin asked, "What?"

They ignored him.

Trent asked Jen, "Really, what is this?"

Jen snorted. She said, "It's a Crossover Ceremony. You should know this. Six lanterns in a circle… the feast with the webbing at the end…"

"Shh!" Natalie said.

Trent looked out to the lit clearing.

Martin groaned.

The professor whispered, "The super people will be here soon. Be quiet. Turn on some cameras. We should lie down in these bushes."

They all dropped to their bellies and wiggled into the bushes near one of the lamps. They could see the clearing perfectly.

Martin hawked and spit. He said, "Fuck. Got puke mouth."

"Shh!" Natalie shushed.

Trent kicked at the frat boy lying beside him.

Martin made a terrible huffing sound. "Hunh hunh huh-huh-huh-hrrraaaaaawwwww!" He puked all over the ground beside Trent.

Gray vomit pooled in the shadowy light of the lantern. Trent tried rolling over, but couldn't move. The puke began spreading out across the ground.

Martin stared at the lamp. Barf hung from his open mouth.

"Do something!" Trent hissed.

The frat boy pointed at the lantern. He whispered, "Look at that sweet glowing ass."

"What?" Trent looked.

A shining super woman stood inside the glass box at the top of a short wooden pole. Her curvy butt lit up like a nuclear lightning bug. Martin couldn't stop staring. Pieces of blubber puke hung off his smiling lips.

"The lamps are chicks with lit-up asses," the frat boy said.

Trent shoved him. "Come *on*! Move over. Your puke is going to get on my pants."

The puddle expanded and ran downhill between the two students. Trent thought he could feel it soaking into his jeans. He thought he'd probably vomit, too.

The professor shushed him.

There was activity at the edge of the clearing.

A paved path bisected the circle of lanterns. Super people from Hero Village came into the light, walking in a slow procession. The leader was in front of the line, and she stopped them all in the center. The group of super people formed a loose semi-circle.

The woman with the baby that Trent saw crying earlier stood in the middle of the super people. She held her infant to her chest. It was swaddled in some sort of shimmery blanket. The woman held her head down, still crying. A super man stood with his arm around her.

Martin whispered, "Holy shit!" He poked Trent and pointed across the clearing.

From out of the shadows of the jungle stepped the other super people of the island.

Trent forgot about the puke, watching the arrival of the villains.

A tall super person in silver was in the lead. His head was like a lit match. He floated above the stones of the path on rocket feet, scorching the rocks.

A frightening procession of villains followed. A ten-foot tall woman crashed out of the jungle behind him, towering over one of the living lanterns. She carried a club made from a petrified tree. An inky, slithering man unwound from the giant's wrist and dropped to the ground. He moved like black mercury across the pathway toward its center.

A cloud of shimmering, buzzing bees swarmed over the clearing and spun like a cyclone down to the ground, forming itself into a beautiful woman in a yellow suit with a black and yellow wasp-striped cape. A demon-faced red guy in a white and blue suit took her hand as he approached the gathering at the center. Smoke shot from his metallic mohawk.

Martin pointed out a voluptuous woman in a black and red suit who slinked out of the shadows. Her outfit exposed most of her un-suited flesh. Her breasts were abnormally large, even for the normally well-endowed super people. Even from their distance, Trent could see her pointy nipples, her patch of glistening pubic hair, and the twinkle in her eye. A handsome blond man in a blue suit with a black spiral on his chest held her hand.

Three giant roaches skittered out of the jungle, each running in opposite directions around the clearing. One scampered right past the group of anthropologists. They came together near the center of the circle and piled up, one atop another. They mooshed and popped into a man-shaped bug wearing a slick, brown-black suit.

The group of villains gathered opposite of the villagers from Hero Village.

Trent asked Jen, "What are *they* doing here?"

"Are you kidding me? A Crossover Ceremony? Come on, Trent." She explained it to him, knowing full-well that he should know it all himself, and being more than a little disappointed in him for not.

Martin listened in.

"Crossover Ceremonies are one of the most complex, private, and debated aspects of the culture of the island. You know that the only thing that separates heroes and villains is the color of their suits. Heroes have red, white, and blue as their costume coloring—nothing more, nothing less. Anyone else is a villain.

"Because super people are born with their suits, and have no control over how they will turn out, sometimes a hero is born to the villains, or vice-versa. When this happens, they have a Crossover Ceremony. The child is given over to its village, Hero Village or Villain Village.

"It rarely works-out that there is a couple from the heroes giving over a villain baby at the same time as a villain couple has a little hero. Usually, there's a waiting period for couples to get an adoptive child from the other village. Sometimes couples opt to not adopt, even after having given up their own infant. Do you remember any of this from class?"

Trent nodded absently. He realized why the woman he'd seen had been crying. Her baby had yellow on his belly. The addition of yellow made the baby a villain. Trent thought about the island's system. He found it ridiculous that something they had no control over, their own birth, labeled them for life. He thought it must be horrifying for any super person to have a child. That poor couple out there, handing their baby over to another family, an entirely different village.

The puke was definitely soaking into his jeans.

Madame Manifestor approached the burning-head villain. They met each other in the direct center of the circle. Thought bubbles expanded and popped. Each leader turned to its tribe and spoke.

The professor whispered, "This is the opening of the ceremony. The leaders are incanting the words of exchange."

The spider woman turned to the hero couple and motioned them to come forward. *Bring the villain!*

They slowly approached, the woman dragging her feet and hunching against her super husband. The super man carried her along.

Flame-Head motioned toward his people, and a couple

came forward. It was the woman with the revealing suit and her blue-suited husband.

Martin said, "Lucky kid."

The couples and the leaders stood in the center of the circle. The woman with the baby held it close to her blue chest.

Madame Manifestor spoke to the hero couple. It was a wide, fat speech bubble that hung in the air for a long time. Trent couldn't read it all, but it seemed very formal. Once it popped, the spider woman held out her hands to take the baby.

The super woman didn't want to hand it over. She shook her head.

Her husband spoke to her. *It is time.*

She shook her head.

The super man took the baby from her and handed it over to their leader. The woman buried her face in her husband's chest.

Madame Manifestor held the baby up to her villagers and spoke another fat bubble that lingered. *This child, born in Hero Village, is truly a villain. Let this baby be with its kind forevermore.*

She turned to the flaming leader of the villains and handed him the swaddled infant.

The villain took the baby and held it up for his villagers. He spoke to them in a long lasting speech bubble, and then handed the baby to the woman of the villain couple.

The moment that the baby was in the voluptuous woman's hands, the crying hero woman went berserk. A jagged speech bubble shot from her mouth. *NO!*

She erupted in a spinning vortex of white energy and shot into the air.

The super woman hung above the clearing, howling and waving her arms around. Blackness blotted out the stars behind her, and electricity arched over her glowing white head. She began gathering a ball of lightning between her hands.

Jen whisper-hissed, "She's going to kill someone!"

The woman's husband flew into the air, barreling into his anguished wife. He shouted a spiky bubble, *Twister! Stop!*

She took his hit and smashed him in the face with her crackling sphere of energy. The man crashed to the ground.

Thick black tentacles shot from the hero crowd and wrapped themselves around the grieving woman in the sky. They pulled her slowly down.

Tree tops whipped around in a tempest. The air grew heavy. *Let me go!*

Twister struggled with her bonds just as another super woman flew up beside her and hit her square in the jaw.

The grieving super woman exploded in a thunderous release of plasma—blasting the tentacles from her and sending the other woman flying into the jungle. *That's my baby!* Twister spun in a tight circle, and the vortex she created began uprooting trees from the edge of the clearing.

A spinning tree trunk whacked into the forest just behind the huddled anthropologists. Jen screamed, and Trent slapped his hand over her mouth.

A super hero flying past turned at the sound of Jen's shout. He floated near them for a moment, surveying the forest, but soon returned to the scuffle.

Twister spun, gathering chunks of earth and forest in her whirling wind.

A tremendous jagged speech bubble erupted from Madam Manifestor, *Stop this now!* A thick web shot from her spinneret ass and wrapped itself around the frantic hero in the sky. She cocooned the woman.

The anguished mother slammed into the hard-packed dirt of the circle.

Heroes settled down. Some went to retrieve the wrapped up heroine. Others helped her husband to his feet.

The villains observed the scene, but did not respond. They stood calmly and allowed the heroes to rein the woman in.

When it was over, the two leaders exchanged a few more bubbles. Then the villain leader addressed the smiling villain couple and his people, and they all filed out of the circle.

The professor said to his students, "Let's get out of here."

They went quietly back to camp. No one spoke as they crawled into their tents. Trent tried to not think about what they'd just seen so that his dreams would be happy.

He awoke several times in the night to screams that may or may not have happened.

Chapter Five

Trent awoke in his sun-heated oven tent. He tumbled out before he baked and found the other students already up, eating breakfast at the campfire.

Jen said, "Good morning, sleepyhead."

He raised his toiletry bag in greeting and staggered toward the latrine.

Martin harassed him as soon as he returned. "Hey, Trent, today's the day! I can't wait to get assigned one of those super fine women to follow around all day. Best class ever, right, dude?"

Trent asked, "Is there still strawberry oatmeal?" He wandered toward the food locker.

The professor and Natalie showed up as Trent was boiling water.

"I've been to the village this morning, students. Things there are normal. We were not noticed last night." Professor Topper clapped his hands and looked around. "If you all want to hurry up with your breakfast and gather your equipment, we should be getting to assignments soon.

"Since you'll be studying super people as they go about their daily business, you should keep in mind the dangers of the jungles that are outlined in your orientation packets and waivers—which I'm sure you've all read in great detail. These include a variety of poisonous plants, rip tides, geysers, insects, and dangerous animals like the island panda and giant island boar. Those boars are vicious, angry monsters. Pray you have a super person near you if you run into one. But you shouldn't, there aren't many of them and they generally stay to the north of the island."

The young field researchers looked around at each other. Martin laughed nervously.

Trent added nearly all of the hot water to his tin cup of powdered oatmeal. He put too much in and ended up drinking it all lukewarm and crunchy. He packed the gear he would need for a day of study in the field—laptop, binoculars, balloons and markers, water, pens, pencils, and a notebook.

The professor took the students to the village for their first day of individual field study.

The group stood near the well and looked around at the villagers going about their day. Professor Topper sized up super people.

"Jen," said the professor, "That is your subject." He pointed across the square to a tall, handsome super hero in a red suit with a blue cape. On his massive chest was a white thumbs-up symbol.

The super man stood in the center of a crowd who'd gathered to watch him juggling burning boulders. He tossed flaming rocks the size of vans into the air, smiling, while speech bubbles slipped out from between his happy lips.

Jen said, "Thank you, Professor! You won't be disappointed."

"I'm sure I won't, Jen."

She smiled at Trent, said, "Good luck!" and walked off toward the hero, taking notes.

Martin tugged at the professor's shirt. He said, "I'm gonna get set up with a female, right?"

Gazing around at the villagers, the professor told him, "Oh, sure, if you'd like. How about…that one, right there."

Trent and Martin looked to where their teacher pointed.

Martin said, "No, I said a female."

The villager was a large, round, lumpy sort of person in a dirty white suit with red and white stripes running up its sides, emphasizing the enormity of the woman's gut. She sat in the dirt and picked stuff from her jagged teeth. Clotted grease slopped over the super woman's ham-sized breasts which drooped over the sides of her heaving bovine body. Her face and arms were a constantly swirling, swampy sort of substance. Objects churned just under the surface of her oil-slick skin. The woman's hair clung to the sides of her head in a greasy mop. Long, pointed, doggish teeth grimaced behind giant slug lips. Viscous goo dripped out of her gaping cave-mouth. Little puffs of dust escaped from under her shaking tree-trunk thighs—she was constantly farting.

The super blob sat near a pile of chopped-up whale carcass. Tattered black skin hung off yellow hunks of whale. Martin's subject was shoving head-sized chunks of the meat into her mouth. Super people kept their distance from her, but one young girl tossed a half-eaten mango on the scrap pile while the students watched.

Professor Topper said, "She's female, Martin. Off you go! Now remember, your job is to uncover as many of your subject's super powers as possible. And you also need to report on her general behaviors—her daily routines. But keep your distance for now."

"Yeah. Yeah. But, really? What's she doing over there?"

The professor gave the frat boy a nudge in the back. "Eating, Martin. Now go on."

Natalie said, "Have fun, Marty."

Martin scowled at her and stalked off toward his subject.

Trent hid his laughter by pretending to cough.

The professor said, "Trent, I don't think we're going to find your subject here. Why don't we take a little stroll and see who we can find for you."

"Oh. Okay," Trent looked around at all the perfectly acceptable subjects wandering around the square and followed the professor.

They came to a hut with a young boy sitting in the dirt outside of it, letting a caterpillar wander over his hands. It was the bald kid from dinner.

His little head shone in the sun.

The professor said, "There's your villager, Trent." He

pointed at the boy.

Trent said, "What? Are you sure, Professor? I mean, he's a kid. He might be kind of boring."

Natalie said, "No one is boring in anthropology, Trent. And the same age sets don't apply here as they do in our society. Being a kid isn't that much different than being an adult, other than their powers not being completely developed."

The professor agreed. He said, "This is your subject, Trent. Figure out his powers, let us in on his daily life, what makes the little guy tick. And have a great time!"

Trent watched the kid play with the bug. He asked, "Are you sure?" But Professor Topper and Natalie were gone.

Trent slumped against a tree and pulled out his notebook.

The little super hero ignored Trent, turning his hands over and over to provide a continuous track for the caterpillar.

Chapter Six

Trent sat on a rock watching the bald kid. They'd left the village almost immediately after the professor ditched him. The kid wandered away into the jungle and now ran around in the evening surf.

The child's suit interested Trent. It was the only thing that did. It was a white suit with just two very thin lines of blue and red around his waist. His chest emblem was a white square, outlined with a slight blue line. In the middle of the square were red squiggles. So that's what Trent called the kid—Squiggles.

Trent thought that Squiggles had to be the most boring super person in the village. He followed the kid for seven hours and hadn't seen the boy use a single power. All Squiggles had done was poke things with sticks, play with bugs, and play in mud. Trent thought maybe his power was boring people to death. He almost wrote that down in his notebook.

He read over his notes of the day:

Friday, June 3rd

9:42 AM—Kid has spent half an hour watching caterpillar crawl. Well, half an hour since I've been observing him.

10:12 AM—Followed kid to beach. Kid poking dead fish with stick.

11:21 AM—Kid is still poking fish.

1:02 PM:—Back in village at kid's hut. Kid is eating bugs or something. I'm going to call him Squiggles because of his chest emblem.

1:35 PM—In the jungle. Walked about five miles uphill. Kid is sitting in a mud puddle. He has a big folded leaf tied to his head with grass—like a hat, or mask, or something.

2:02 PM—Still in mud puddle. I think I fell asleep. It IS a mask on his head. It has eye-holes which he put fruit rinds in so they look like big, bugged-out eyes. It looks like he's looking me.

3:33 PM—I know I fell asleep. Couldn't find kid. Hunted around and found him further up the hill in a different mud puddle. He's been pulling rocks out of the muck and building a castle for worms. He's found a lot of worms.

4:32 PM—At the beach. Kid is splashing around, getting mud off. Ran away from a jellyfish.

4:45 PM—Squiggles is the most boring bald kid I've ever seen.

Trent left the kid in the surf and went back to camp.

He found Jen and Martin there, washing balloons. He joined them.

"Don't you have any balloons to wash?" Jen asked. She had a pile of shriveled up balloons with black on them at her feet.

Martin looked up. He held a wad of used balloons. He said, "I lost most of mine. I've only got about ten left."

Jen said, "Well if you didn't waste so many with ridiculous nonsense, you'd have more."

Trent said, "I didn't use any today. I still have the ones from the first day. I can reuse them if I ever need to try and communicate. My guy is that little bald kid from dinner. The one who doesn't do anything."

"You mean, doesn't use his powers often?" Jen asked.

Trent said, "He doesn't have powers."

Jen stopped washing her balloon. "He has to have powers. You just haven't found them yet. You know, they could be subtle, like how Fabulous Man has that cute little power of turning rocks to chocolate. Or when he makes music by rubbing his eyelashes together. And if you consider hilarity a super power, there's that, too."

"You're so in love with your super dude," Martin said.

Jen blushed. She went back to washing her balloons.

Trent said, "What all can your super person do, Martin?"

"You mean besides eating half-a-whale in five minutes, super-stench, and mega-fart power? Nothing else so far."

Jen asked, "Is that why you spent more time following Heat Vixen around all day?"

"I… That's… shut up, Jen."

Trent left them to wash their balloons. He slipped into his tent before the professor noticed he'd returned. He didn't want to have to face him with a day of nothing to report.

Chapter Seven

Trent flipped through the pages of his notebook. It contained two days record of nearly the exact same thing: poking dead things and playing with bugs. Two days of the most boring subject on the island. Plus several other pages filled with doodles. He liked to have the notebook for sketching more than anything.

Natalie walked over to him and tapped the top of his notebook with her pencil. "Today is the day, Trent. You're going to have to find at least one super power from that kid. You'll have to make contact with him today—communicate with him and learn his powers."

He looked up. "What?"

"Oh come on, Trent. Even Martin has exchanged speech bubbles with his subject."

"That was just about sharing food with him."

"At any rate, you're the only one who hasn't discovered a single power from your villager. You're failing, Trent. Get out there and get on it." Natalie pushed her glasses up and sauntered away.

Trent collected his equipment.

Jen came by as he was checking the charge on his laptop. She said, "I heard some of that with Natalie. Don't worry about it. I'm sure when you talk to the little guy you'll learn what his powers are."

"Thanks," Trent said. He didn't look forward to talking to the kid, but he thought it was kind of Jen to say such things.

Trent went to find Squiggles.

Of course, he was difficult to find. It took Trent about

an hour to locate him. He was down the beach, dragging seaweed around on the sand. But he climbed over the dunes just as Trent approached him.

Trent followed cautiously.

Squiggles headed into the jungle. Trent trailed him back to his favorite mud puddle. This time the kid was combining sitting in mud and poking dead things with a stick. There was a lump of something furry at the edge of the puddle. The super kid jabbed at it.

Trent crouched beside a tree just down the creek from the kid and took a balloon and marker from his pocket.

Squiggles had never paid any attention to Trent. The student worried he might spook him if he approached too quickly. He adjusted his backpack and crept up the creek bed. The boy stopped poking and looked up. Trent sat down.

The boy went back to poking the dead thing. Trent made his way closer.

Being an anthropology student, Trent knew that mimicry could help him relate to his study subject. So Trent found a long stick and edged closer to the boy. He sat beside the puddle and poked at the fur blob.

The super kid looked at Trent. It was the closest the two had been together, and Trent got a good look at the child's eyes. His irises were shades of gray.

Trent inflated his balloon.

The boy watched him.

He scribbled, *Hi, I'm Trent.* and held the balloon to his face.

The boy spoke. His bubble inflated and a big bold question mark appeared. The bubble was different than any Trent had seen. It was almost the jagged bubble that meant surprise or anger. There were points on it, but they curved around the bubble, like a pinwheel. His speech bubbles gave the impression of spinning.

Trent blew up another balloon and wrote on it. It read, *My name is Trent. What's yours?*

Squiggles answered, *?* inside one of those dynamic bubbles.

Another balloon. *What is your name?*

The kid answered with another question mark.

Trent sighed. "Really?" He shook his head.

Squiggles smiled at him. *?*

Trent went through seventeen balloons just trying to elicit a different response. The kid only answered with a big question mark inside his weird speech bubble. After nearly two hours of trying to communicate, Trent gave up and went back to observing the kid from a distance.

The boy eventually wandered back to the village.

Trent returned to camp.

He had an hour there all by himself. He rehydrated soup and reviewed his notes about Squiggles. Then Natalie showed up. She made a beeline for his hammock.

"Well? How did it go?" she asked.

Trent stammered. "Well, uh. Well, we exchanged speech bubbles about six times."

She stared down at him. "And?"

"And?"

"What are his powers? What can he do?"

"Oh. Well. I. It's just that… Um."

"You still don't know?"

Trent just looked at her.

She said, "Well you'd better get your act together, Trent. You'll be playing a lot of catch-up because you're in for a lot more work. You're about to be assigned your second super person to observe."

"Crap."

"Exactly," Natalie said. She went to her own tent, shaking her head.

Trent closed his eyes and let the hammock rock him. Another super person. And he had no clue about his first one other than he was deficient or something. When the other students came drifting back to camp, Trent pretended to be asleep. He sneaked into his tent while everyone was eating dinner. No one came looking for him.

Chapter Eight

Trent awoke from a dream about eating his way out of a coagulated pudding bear. The professor was shouting, "Everyone up! Everyone up!"

By the time Trent made it out of his tent, the rest of the group was gathered around the fire. Trent opted to wait to visit the latrine.

Professor Topper stood at his field table with Natalie.

The teacher addressed his students once Trent arrived. "Today is the day you get your second assigned super person."

Martin whispered to Trent, "Second times's a charm."

Trent ignored him.

The professor continued, "We're doing things a bit differently this time. I'm going to give you the name of the super person which you'll be studying, and you'll have to go to Villain Village and find them."

Jen asked, "Villain Village?"

"Really?" Trent asked.

Martin said, "Villain girls are hot."

"Yes, Villain Village," the professor told them.

The students looked around at each other. None of them, not even Martin, were comfortable with going off to Villain Village by themselves and finding their subjects by name alone.

Professor Topper said, "The villains are as concerned with us as the heroes are. We're neutral observers. They probably won't pay you much attention at all and most likely won't perceive you as enemies. You'll be fine."

"*Most likely?*" said Martin.

Natalie handed the professor a piece of paper.

He said, "Here are the names of your villains. Jen, you'll be observing Fuzzy Nightmare."

Jen said, "Is that a boy or a girl?"

The professor said, "Martin, you've got The Detonator."

The frat boy muttered, "That does *not* sound like a villainous hottie."

"So, the two of you can just head to the village and find your subjects. Trent, your villain is a bit of a different story."

Trent looked around at his fellow students and then back to the professor. Natalie was smiling at him and he didn't like that one bit.

The professor said, "Trent, you've got Death Killer."

"Death Killer?" Trent asked.

"Death Killer!" said Martin.

"Yes, Death Killer," said Professor Topper. "He's an interesting individual. He doesn't live in the village, but rather on his own at the top of Shark Tooth Mountain. You'll have to go there to find him, but it shouldn't be too big of a problem for you. I've got confidence."

"Death Killer?" Trent asked.

"Natalie will fill you in on how to find him," the professor told him. To the group he said, "So gather your equipment, make sure your laptops are all charged up. I expect some decent preliminary reports on these villains. And have fun!"

The professor went into his tent with Natalie.

Martin said, "Fun? With a villain named The Detonator? What the hell happened here?" He wandered off.

Jen said to Trent, "I can't believe Topper gave you Death Killer!"

Trent said, "Uh. Yeah."

"Because, I've heard about him. Fabulous Man says he's the most feared of all the villains. Even the other villains are afraid him, so bad that they're afraid to let him live with *them*. I can't believe the professor would give such a difficult subject to *you*." Jen walked away.

Trent watched her go.

Natalie silently appeared beside him. He jumped.

She handed him a folded up piece of paper and said, "Here's a map to Shark Tooth Mountain. It might take a while to get to the top, so you should probably get going." She pushed her glasses up and smiled. She went back to the professor's tent.

Trent stood and looked at the paper in his hand. He went to pee and gather his equipment.

The professor called them all together again as they were ambling out of camp. He said, "Look, I really don't want you to worry about this assignment. The villains are just super people, just like the heroes. In fact, you all know Heat Vixen. Well, she's a Crossover. She was born in Villain Village. And you all get along just fine with her, right? My point is—"

He was interrupted by the sound of jets coming from the sky behind them.

Five huge aircraft flew over in tight formation. The sound of their engines shook the island below them.

"Fighter planes?" Natalie yelled.

"Hell no!" shouted Martin. "Those are goddamn cyber-troopers!" He shielded his eyes from the sun with a shaky hand. "At least third generation—with quadratic afterburners and hexagonal woven armor."

The craft passed over them, roaring across the sky toward the northern part of the island.

"Cyber-troopers?" Jen asked.

"Are you fuckin' serious?!" Martin said. He looked to Trent for support.

Trent shrugged. He knew about cyber-troopers, but only that they existed. He was pretty sure Jen should know what they were.

Martin recited, "Cyber-troopers. The TROOPS! Only the biggest and baddest of all modern weaponry combined with the highest technology available. These things are not only the Cadillac of weaponized vehicles, but they're the Porsche of computer brains *and* the Mack truck of toughness.

"High-tension circuitry blended with next-gen weaponry and propulsion systems from the freakin' future! Those babies are what you call, *the shit*! I can't believe we were that close to goddamned cyber-troopers! Holy damn!"

Jen frowned. "Oookay," she said.

The professor looked to the north. "I wonder where they came from. There's no military bases for hundreds of miles."

"I don't know, but I hope they come back," Martin said.

The professor kept looking at the sky. "Yes. Well… Okay, off you go then, students."

Trent watched the professor watch the sky.

When Natalie made shooing motions at him, he hefted his pack, took a look at his map, and headed toward Shark Tooth Mountain.

Chapter Nine

Trent walked through the jungle. After following Natalie's map for about a mile, he saw the mountain he was looking for—a tall craggy thing with sprouting palms that looked like stray whiskers poking off its pointy face. He tucked the map away and made for the mountain.

The jungle paths were mostly clear of undergrowth. Occasionally, they were choked with vegetation where the sun broke through the canopy, and tropical plants filled natural pavilions. It was in one such sunny circle, not far into his journey, that Trent stumbled upon a super sapien anthropologist's dream. Or nightmare.

Coming into the sun, he happened to look up and see a villain standing in his path, seething.

Trent said, "Uh oh."

The villain had a green and purple suit with a black cape. His huge, square head and massive hands seemed to be made of concrete. His chest emblem was a black cube. He smashed his hands together and a booming clap shook the air. Trent didn't think. He turned and ran.

He sprinted straight into a looming hero, and bounced off him, falling to the ground. The hero was a tall super man in a blue suit with white stripes and a red band around his waist. He had a blue mask covering his eyes. There was a red horse's head across his chest. He was obviously furious.

Trent screamed and scrambled backward, forgetting the villain for a moment. The hero spoke with a huge, jagged bubble. *I know you've done something with my wife, Cinderblock, my old nemesis!*

Trent crammed himself under a fallen tree. The villain

said something Trent couldn't read, and the hero replied with a quick, jagged bubble, *Never!*

The hero leapt over Trent, landed hard on the path, and punched the villain's concrete jaw. The villain flew backward, crashing onto his back with a tremendous thud. He got to his knees and grabbed the end of the log Trent was hiding under. Trent scrambled out. The hero turned and looked at him.

The villain stood, ripping the massive trunk from the ground. He swung it toward Trent and the hero. Trent dove. The hero put his arm up to block the blow, and the tree trunk cracked in half. Splinters shot all around Trent. He yelled, and lurched away.

The hero picked up a huge rock and hefted it while Trent rolled from the scuffle. The student leapt over another log as the hero threw the boulder at Cinderblock. Trent ducked down and the villain demolished the flying stone with his fist. Chunks of rock shot through the trees.

After the rocky rain, Trent poked his head up to see what was happening.

The super men were grappling. Speech bubbles popped off, but Trent was at the wrong angle to read them.

Cinderblock broke free of the hero's grip, clapped his rocky hands on either side of the hero's head, and whipped around in a circle, tossing his nemesis into the log Trent was hiding behind. The rotted tree trunk shattered as the hero flew through it, and Trent dove for the opposite side of the path.

He came to his feet at the same time as the hero, facing the villain.

A thick, jagged thought bubble shot out of Cinderblock's cracked mouth. It read, *You cannot win against me, Mustang Tornado.*

Mustang Tornado stared at the villain, and lasers shot from his eyes. Twin beams of sizzling red energy burst from the hero and blasted straight into Cinderblock's chunky head. Black smoke hissed off the villain's face. Trent leapt behind a moss-covered boulder alongside the trail.

The concrete man raised his hands. Diamond-shaped

rocks flew from his palms, splattering into Mustang Tornado, and staggering the hero backward. Stone bullets ricocheted off of Trent's boulder and stuck into trees.

Trent cowered, screaming. He looked at the hero. One of the crusty projectiles buried itself into Mustang Tornado's right eye. There was a flash of orange fire and an explosion. The super man let out a long, jagged bubble of pain, *Yeeaaaarrrrgh!* and flew backward into the jungle—the bubble stretching out behind him before it popped.

Cinderblock screamed out a huge, spiky bubble. *Diiiiiiiiie!* He tore off after the fleeing hero.

Trent lay against the rock until the birds started chirping again. Then he got the hell away from the spontaneous battle arena. Once he stopped shaking, he thought about sketching the scene later. It certainly made an impression.

When Trent arrived at the mountain, he wished he had a map that told him the easiest ascent. He stood and craned his neck backward, gaping up at the imposing peak. *Are they fucking serious?*

He let his pack slide off his back. He thought about just spending the day right where he stood and saying that he never even saw Death Killer. Then he thought about his failure with Squiggles, and Natalie's evil smile, and the fact that he had to do *something* while he was on the island. If he didn't, the professor would surely have something to say about his performance when it came time for grades.

But he was also worried about his safety. He was concerned for his equipment, too. Trent looked at his pack, with the laptop in its pouch, the binoculars hanging off, and the camera he hadn't used. It would be a climb to get to the top, and if he bashed that laptop, he'd be ruined. He'd been taking notes by hand all week, anyway. Trent decided to stash his pack and climb up without its weight. He tucked it into a hollow log.

"Okay. I can do this," Trent said. He slipped his notebook into his pocket and started climbing.

Trent reached the top two hours later. At the end of his trek, he realized that there was a fairly easy way up—a pathway cut into the mountainside that even included stair-steps.

No one was on top of the mountain.

Not only was no one in sight, but there was no indication that anyone lived there. No hut. No cave. Just rocky ground and rocky spires surrounding it. The mountaintop was flat and wide. There were a few trees and some clumps of bushes scattered among rocks, but it was mostly grass surrounded by tall spires of solid stone.

Once he caught his breath, Trent took a better look around. He explored the summit, poking his head in crevices and crannies but found nothing.

"Fuck this."

As Trent psyched himself up for the climb down, hoping that the path he'd found was going to make it easy, he noticed a strange creature clinging to the top of one of the rock spires. It looked like a huge bird, or a lizard, or maybe a pterodactyl. It perched on the rock, looking out off the mountain top. Trent decided to get a closer look.

He crept toward the creature.

When Trent was within twenty feet of its perch, he realized his mistake. It was not a giant bird, lizard, or even pterodactyl. It was Death Killer. And he was more frightening than all of those things combined.

"Shit," he whispered.

Death Killer was the color of a bruise. Eggplant purple chest bleeding into dark blue, green, and yellow toward his extremities, like he was punched in the whole body as a baby. He had no cape. His head, hands and feet were black. He clung to the rocks with long, terrible toes like thick black centipedes, standing against the blue sky in half-shadow. He was the largest super person Trent had seen. Horns curled off of the villain's shoulders and pointed from his head in haphazard rows from front to back. Tiny fountains of flame shot from them intermittently and they smoldered with thin lines of wispy smoke, like hair.

Trent cowered below the craggy outcropping, praying that the villain hadn't seen him. He wanted to run, but he also did not want to move. Finally, he crept backward until he came to a jagged boulder and he slid behind it.

Peering around the rock, Trent watched Death Killer stretch his body and fly off into the air. The student remained behind the rock, letting the scene sink-in.

He thought, *I'm supposed to talk to him?*

Trent learned two things about his subject: Death Killer could fly, and the villain was the most frightening creature he'd ever seen.

The shaken student scrambled down the path to the foot of the mountain, retrieved his pack, and headed back to camp. Trent was frightened about the prospect of observing Death Killer, but took small solace that at least he'd have a super power to report to the professor.

Chapter Ten

A thundering sound from the sky shook the camp. A helicopter flew overhead, rousing the anthropologists from their tents. It was a military gunship, loaded with missiles and a soldier with a big machine gun. Possessed by some ancient monkey-instinct, Trent fell out of his tent and scrambled toward the fire pit.

Martin whooped, stumbling in his tighty-whities with his hair plastered with drool. He shielded his eyes from the sun and watched the chopper.

After it passed, the professor shouted, "What is a military helicopter doing here?!"

Lightning Ray and Heat Vixen sat beside the professor. No one said anything.

Professor Topper filled a balloon with his air gun and scribbled on it. He held it up, *Lightning Ray, what's with that military helicopter?*

What do you mean?

What are they doing?

The super man shrugged. *Whatever the unmasked do.*

The professor frowned. He announced, "Well I'm going to go investigate. Maybe I can find where the helicopter landed. First those cyber-things and now this."

"Cyber-troopers," Martin corrected.

"You really want to do that, Professor?" Jen asked.

"Of course I do, Jennifer. There is no room for the military on this island, and I intend to discover what they're doing here." He stalked into his tent with Natalie behind him.

The super heroes looked at each other with bemusement and wandered off toward their village.

The professor came out of his tent slinging a backpack over his shoulders. "If you want to come with me, come now," he told them. And he sped off down the trail, following the helicopter's path. Natalie marched beside him.

Martin said, "I'm in!" and ran after him.

Jen and Trent looked at each other and shrugged. They hurried to catch up to the others.

They trekked for a few hours and settled into an easy pace, not paying much attention to their surroundings. They tromped into a clearing filled with tall grass. Trent had just started worrying about hidden animals when he was startled by a deep, gut-shaking, "Halt!"

Everyone stopped.

Trent looked up and shouted, "Whoa!"

Giant robots stood in the trail ahead of them. Cyber-troopers flanked a group of men in camouflage. The cyber soldiers stood nine feet tall—gleaming, armored, man-shaped robots—the new soldiers, laborers, spacemen, underwater explorers, and tundra trailblazers.

Trent thought of the news reports he'd seen on the technology. Cyber-troopers were mega-soldiers first and foremost. He stared up at the huge robots with their rail-gun fists, flame-throwing nozzles, hexagonal armor, and black faceplates. Trent didn't like them.

Martin loved them. He said, "These are fifth generation!"

"Shh!" said Jen.

The professor addressed the men. "Hello. I'm Professor Topper."

A tall soldier with gray hair and steel blue eyes stepped forward and looked them up and down. He puffed on the chewed-up cigar hanging from his cracked lips. He said, "I know who you are, Topper. I know all the rest of you, too."

The students looked around at each other.

The soldier continued, "I pay attention to the happenings

of this island. I'm in charge of it."

The professor grew visibly red. His hands twitched at his sides. He glanced around at the group of soldiers, and the cyber-warriors. He said, "You're *in charge* of it? I'm sorry, but that's simply not true. This island is protected by international law. No country has claim to it."

The soldier smiled. It wasn't a caring smile, or even one that said, *it's okay, stupid, let me enlighten you*. It was a mean smile. He said, "For the record, my name is Colonel Shank. I'm in command of this island."

"That's just ridiculous."

The colonel chuckled flatly. "It's true. The safekeeping and proper functioning of the military facilities on this island are my responsibility."

"Military facilities?"

"We occupy a large part of this island. As a matter of fact, you've been on restricted property since you set up camp. So now you're going to turn around and head back the way you came. Then you're going to move your camp away from our inclusion zone."

"Excuse me?" the professor was fuming. His face flushed nearly purple. Natalie put her hand on his shoulder.

Colonel Shank smiled his terrible smile and pulled a long piece of paper out of his back pocket. He flipped open a map of the island and showed it to the anthropologists. Most of the map was shaded red.

The military man told them, "The red is restricted space. No civilians."

Professor Topper yelled, "Our camp is in the red zone! You can't be serious. Most of the island is marked-off. You have no right. Don't you understand that there are protected tribes of super people here? Why is this the first I've heard of this? You can't be flying around in helicopters over their villages. You can't have your big robots stomping and flying and shooting their guns. This island is protected by the U.N. You are violating laws, here, Colonel, and destroying indigenous cultures. This is beyond outrageous."

The colonel shrugged, "I know who's on the island,

Perfesser. Those damned capebacks are the reason we're here. The restricted zone is for your safety. We are here under order to assure the safety of the surrounding islands, countries, and peoples."

"What are you talking about?" the professor asked.

"Some radioactive super primitive blew himself up last year. We're here to clean up the radiation."

"What?"

"That's right. Flyin' monkey splattered his radioactive guts all over everything. Trees, water, beach… Me and my boys," he motioned to the cyber-troopers who twitched their guns—spinning their gyros and sparking their reactors, "have a hell of a job to do. And we don't need any namby-pamby capeback lovers running around getting themselves radiation sickness. Got it?"

The professor said nothing. He stared at the map that the colonel held.

Martin asked, "What sort of rounds are in those spinner guns, Colonel?"

Shank looked the frat boy up and down. He didn't answer.

Professor Topper said, "I wasn't informed of any radiation. Or of a military base. Our study has been planned for over a year. I would expect someone to warn me about us coming here. Perhaps explain the possible danger. Maybe give us the same map you have."

"One would expect," the colonel said. "But we wouldn't want an accident like this going public, would we? What would that do to your primitive super island? How much damage do you think CNN and Good Morning America will do to the indigenous cultures when they come to do their stories on exploding nuclear super people?"

Professor Topper looked up at the cyber-soldiers, "You know that if the super people perceive you as a threat, they could easily attack you. And destroy you."

Colonel Shank took the cigar out of his mouth. "We're not worried about that, Perfesser. We're perfectly capable of defending ourselves."

"Beyond the damage that you are doing to these tribes,

and this island, I need to be allowed to do my work. I'll be speaking to my superiors about this. Do you understand that by being here, even if you limit your interactions with the super people, you are changing their way of life? Just your intrusion could change their society. This is an outrage!"

The soldier leaned toward the group. He spoke very quietly and said, "Perfesser, if I were you, I'd cooperate unless you want your whole project to end right here and now."

"You couldn't do that."

The colonel looked him straight in the eyes and said, "Try me."

Professor Topper stared at the military man.

Trent looked at the other soldiers flanked by the cyber-troopers. They all looked angry.

Colonel Shank shoved the map at the professor. "Take this. If you come on restricted area again, I'll have your study revoked." He clamped his cigar in his teeth and frowned.

The solider walked back to his entourage, and they followed him into the tall grass. The cyber-soldiers went last, tromping the grass down so that the anthropologists caught a glimpse of the helicopter and the base beyond it.

Trent saw three squat, rectangular buildings through the trees.

The colonel yelled back at them, "Go back to your camp. But move it by tomorrow."

The professor turned and stomped back the way they'd come without a word. His students followed.

Chapter Eleven

There were super heroes sitting around the table when the group got back. They all disappeared in their own super ways—flying off, teleporting, going invisible, becoming a gazelle—when they heard the anthropologists return. Most of the peanut butter was gone.

"Have my study revoked. That goon." The professor stalked between his tent and the table. "Revoke my study."

Martin said to Trent, "Did you *see* those cyber-troopers? Holy shit, man! Those were brand-new, off-the-line man-machines. Fuckin' A, dude. I'd love to see those babies in action."

Jen said, "Martin, have you bathed today?"

"What?" He looked around nervously. "Yeah, I know. It's that sludge monster the professor teamed me up with. I'm startin' to smell like her. I'm about ready to just ditch her completely."

Jen frowned and ducked into her tent.

Trent went to investigate the status of the peanut butter and worry a little about camping in radiation.

The professor ranted. "Radiation! Bah! There's no radiation. Why aren't there signs? Why wasn't I informed before we arrived?"

"Well, the colonel said they don't want to draw attention to it, sir," Natalie said.

"Well I don't care what he said. He can't tell me where I can and can't go on this island. I can go wherever I want. I *will* go wherever I want." Professor Topper stalked into his tent.

Natalie followed him inside.

Trent picked up an empty peanut butter jar. He wondered if they'd walked through irradiated areas. He wondered if he'd brushed up against a nuclear plant, or breathed a cloud of alpha radiation. Trent was certain he'd stay away from the restricted area. He rummaged for a new jar of peanut butter and some honey.

The anthropologists gathered and took sandwiches as Trent put them together. They sat around the table.

"I want to go back and see those cyber-troopers," Martin said.

"You will not be going back there," the professor told him.

Jen said, "We do need to get word out somehow about this, at least to the University. Right, Professor?"

A little hero girl appeared beside Martin and snatched the sandwich from his hands. She blinked out of existence as quickly as she popped in.

"What the hell?" Martin looked around for the girl and his sandwich. No one seemed to care about it.

The professor said, "The University, yes." He took a bite of his sandwich and spaced-out in thought.

Trent said, "We've got to pack up camp."

"Natalie will start on that soon," Topper said absently.

Martin grabbed another sandwich and looked around nervously. He guardedly took a bite. As he was about to take another, the girl showed up out of thin air and grabbed the sandwich. She disappeared.

"Damnit!" Martin yelled.

The others looked over to him apathetically and went back to talking about the soldiers.

"Those buildings looked like they'd been there a while," Trent said.

"Yes," said the professor, "I thought the same thing."

"I hope we didn't walk through radiation," said Jen.

"According to the map, we're in it now," the professor answered.

Martin huddled over his plate, taking his last sandwich in hand. He glared around the camp.

When nothing happened for a while, and everyone else ate their food in peace, Martin relaxed just a tiny bit. The little super hero popped back in front of the frat boy. She grabbed him by his arms and snapped out of sight, taking Martin with her. The sandwich fell to the table.

They reappeared twenty feet away. The girl dumped Martin in the dust and teleported back. She smiled at the other students as she took Martin's sandwich and vanished.

"What the *fuck*!" Martin yelled. He sat on his butt for awhile trying not to notice that most everyone was laughing at him. Then he wandered toward the beach.

Trent finished his sandwich while the professor ranted about precedent, exploitation, and nuclear radiation affecting babies in Hawaii and Idaho. He watched Natalie start cleaning the kitchen area.

Not long after, everyone joined her in packing their own gear—save their tents and sleeping bags—and added it to her growing pile. Natalie would relocate it all.

The next day, after helping set up a new camp, Trent followed Squiggles. He went to the mango orchard and then down to the tide pools. He poked at things with sticks. He sat in mud. And then he started walking down a path that led toward the restricted area.

Trent followed along the path until he was certain that the kid had entered the off-limits zone. Trent didn't continue. He wondered about radiation and what it does to super children. Shivering, he turned and went back to the new camp site.

Chapter Twelve

Trent lay against an outcropping of rock at the top of Shark Tooth Mountain. He watched Death Killer in the distance. He sketched in his notebook. He'd left his laptop behind, as it had been acting strange the day before—turning off randomly. And it was cathartic to draw the scenes he witnessed during the day.

Death Killer was using fire breath to roast a raccoon. The villain dispatched the little critter with bursts of lasers from his eyes. He skinned it with a jerking motion, scooped out its guts and flung them out to sea, held the thing up and started blasting it with fire from his mouth.

Trent didn't want to get closer to the villain than he was, but before he left camp that morning Natalie told him that he had to attempt contact with Death Killer that day. That meant that he had to pull himself from his hiding place. He told himself, "Okay, Trent. This is it."

He got up and started slowly toward the super man. Trent dodged between boulders and spires, ducking behind them as he approached. Soon nothing but flat space, one clump of trees, and a few bushes separated the student from the super villain.

Trent hid behind the last big rock. He began worrying about how to get Death Killer's attention without getting blasted by fire. He thought about the raccoon. He poked his head around the boulder and watched the villain eat.

Death Killer bit into the charred raccoon's head. Brains burst from the popping skull, and splashed onto the villain's face. He chewed, grinding bones between his pointed teeth, and dripping brains on his chin and upper body. The super man pulled a string of steaming headguts off his shoulder and slurped it like a noodle.

Trent nearly vomited. He began backing away, tucking his notebook in his pants. *Fuck this*, he thought. He turned to run and tripped. "Ooof!"

Death Killer heard him.

The super man's head snapped around. He dropped the barbequed beastie and flew toward Trent.

Scuttling backward like an epileptic crab, Trent got his first close look at the super villain. Time slowed as the muscle-bound maniac stood over him.

Two rows of vampire teeth dripped with gore. Red eyes glowed from behind his dark mask. Death Killer's hands crackled with plasma. Below his knee, studs and spikes adorned his boots, his long, segmented, centipede toes stuck through their steel tips. A thin red line outlined a black sun-shaped emblem on his chest. White bones protruded from his spine like shark-fin thorns.

The villain drained Trent's strength with his burning presence. It was like the rest of the world swirled away, was flushed out of reality, and the only things left were Trent and this horrible thing barreling down on him. Trent was sure he was peeing his pants.

"Heh...Hel...Hel...Hell!"

Death Killer telepathically slammed the student backward, knocking him to the ground with the energy of thought.

Trent tried his crab shuffle through the dirt again. The super man roared above him. Trent wanted to close his eyes, but couldn't. He watched Death Killer transform.

The villain grew. He stretched up and filled out, and soon towered over Trent. He howled.

Trent screamed and threw his hands up over his face. Dust choked him. "Don't kill me!"

The building-sized super man raised his enormous foot over the student. Trent cowered as the super monster prepared to crush him under his huge centipede toes. But the villain didn't stomp him. Giant-sized Death Killer dug his disgustingly long toes into the ground all around Trent, imprisoning him in foot-jail.

It smelled like a bucket of dead worms inside the clawed foot. Jagged speech bubbles blasted down toward Trent, but he only caught glimpses of white and heard their wet popping all around him. Trent tried to wiggle between two of the armored toes.

Giant Death Killer closed his foot-fist. He scooped Trent up in his claws and brought his leg to his huge villain face to examine the tiny creature he'd trapped.

Trent managed to pull out a balloon and his marker. As he rolled around in his clawed cage, he tried to blow up the balloon but kept falling over. "Crap crap crap crap!"

The giant's eyes glowed red, but their irises were dark blue. A tremendous, jagged scar cut through the thick mask-flesh along his right cheek to the top of his head. There were ridges across the bridge of the villain's nose. His pointed teeth had hollow tips, like hypodermic needles. Heavy, dank breath rushed over Trent as he pushed himself into the hard sole of the creature's foot and inflated the balloon. He scribbled on it. *I'm Trent! Please don't kill!*

The villain's breath grew hot. Lighter fluid vapors filled the choking air. Trent started screaming. He wriggled his way between two of the huge toes and found himself eye-to-tremendous-eye with Death Killer. Trent let go of his balloon. It shot off between gigantic toes.

The huge villain blasted out another jagged thought bubble—this one the size of a billboard—straight at the tiny student. The bubbled enveloped Trent, bursting around him and thumping his ears with a sonic boom.

Trent kept screaming.

Death Killer flung him across the top of the mountain.

The student bounced along the ground, cartwheeling over clumps of grass and into a bush. He got up and ran without looking back, practically jumping down the mountain on bashed and battered legs.

Trent kept running until he was out of breath, tripping to a stop at an old mossy stump. He tried to stop shaking. He drank from a stream beside him, washed off the scratches on his arms and legs, and followed the creek to the beach. He sat there and watched the waves break. Eventually he was able to write down some notes.

Saturday, June 11th

Contact with Death Killer. I never want to go back to that mountain. I think I might want to leave the island. He nearly killed me. Big. Really big, ugly death. Raccoon brains. Giant foot jail. I think my shoulder is dislocated.

Confirmed powers:

Fire Breath
Enormous Growth Ability
Jail Toes
Dragon Breath
Telekinesis
Laser Eyes
Super Strength
Blood-Sucking Teeth
Mean Jerkiness
Plasma Hands
Burning Horns

Chapter Thirteen

Martin sat beside Trent at the charging station. Martin was smoldering. His face had black smears all over it. His clothes were tattered and burnt. Trent shook. Neither of them charged their laptops. Trent didn't even have his with him.

Jen skipped into camp holding a pink bunny in her arms. She smiled really big when she saw her fellow students until she noticed Martin's state. She said, "What the heck happened to you?" But she didn't wait for the answer.

Martin opened his mouth and closed it.

Trent let his eyes remain unfocused.

Jen sat down with her bunny and started talking. "I had the *best* day. My villain is *so great*. Seriously. Her name is Fuzzy Nightmare. She is so cute. She's totally pink! I know, can you believe it? Not all just one shade, but all pink. She's fuzzy, and has cat ears. So. Cute. And guess what her power is? It's the best power ever. She turns things into pink bunnies. She can turn anything into pink bunnies. Look at this. It used to be a rock. What are your villains' powers?"

Trent and Martin stared straight ahead.

Jen scratched the bunny and looked up. "Come on, guys, what are their powers?"

Martin sighed. "Self detonation," he said. He brushed his bangs out of his face and they crumbled to ash and blew away. Martin sighed again.

"Hmm." Jen turned to Trent, "So, how's Death Killer?" The bunny squirmed in her arms, and she looked down at it. "You are so *cute*."

Trent stared wide-eyed and unfocused. "He's the scariest fucking dude ever."

"What happened?"

"He wants to kill me."

Jen nodded like she was paying attention and pet her bunny.

Martin got up and left the table in a trance.

"You'll have a better time tomorrow," Jen said.

"I'm not going back there tomorrow."

Jen nodded as she stood. She said, "That's nice. You are the cutest little bunny on all the island. And you were a rock! How cute." She wandered off toward her tent, talking to the bunny.

Trent went to bed.

Chapter Fourteen

Trent followed Squiggles around the next morning and ended up at the village in the early afternoon. He watched the kid drawing in the dirt near the well. Feeling sorry for himself, Trent let his attention wander to the rest of the red, white, and blue village. Just like the first day they'd arrived, there was action going on in the square.

Teenagers wrestled or sat and watched the other teenagers. Two super men were doing an acrobatic display, tossing each other hundreds of feet into the air. There was another boulder juggling competition going on.

He happened to look up just as Jen came flying past hanging on Fabulous Man's back. She waved down at him, giggling. The hero smiled at Trent and nodded before taking off in a long slow bank over the clearing.

Martin had given up on the garbage disposal woman and was following around a tall blond super heroine, holding a balloon to his face.

Trent focused on the boy again. He hadn't moved or looked up from what he was doing. Trent pulled out his laptop and began to take notes.

Sunday, June 12th

Squiggles is as boring as ever.

8:32 AM—I found the kid lining up turtles on their backs at the beach. He ran along tickling their waggling feet. I don't even think turtles are ticklish.

9:03 AM—Squiggles found a dead turtle near the living ones and poked it with a stick. His obsession with dead things may just be because of his age, but I'm starting to suspect that he's fairly depressed with his situation in life. I hope this isn't a sign of him being very disturbed.

9:13 AM—Kid tastes handful of sand.

9:22 AM—Kid tastes seaweed.

9:46 AM—Kid tastes something gray and sticky on beach. What won't he taste?

10:11 AM—First mud puddle of the day. He's only in it to his knees so far.

10:27 AM—Neck-deep. My laptop keeps shutting down. Power is at 85%. I don't know what's up with it.

11:11 AM—Got involved messing with my laptop and lost track of Squiggles. Found him at the edge of the jungle near the beach watching Whalemancer surf. That fish guy makes it look easy. I don't usually see Squiggles paying much attention to the other super people. I wonder how often he watches Whalemancer.

11:40 AM—Kid heads back through jungle toward mud puddles.

11:53 AM—He's not going to puddles. He's headed to restricted area again. I'm not going to follow, but I'll wait and see if he comes back.

3:36 PM—I don't know if the kid came back or not. I was sketching, and drifted off to sleep.

4:02 PM—Squiggles not at puddles.

4:33 PM—Found the kid in village. He's been drawoo UY*D9' ADh dhoaiUUD a(D)fjd BdfsafoHVOBDvdfsa;fadiusUY#@5fdy7/33/3#
HOIHGDSeoiwruqoruasdfguo9782435q23h$#@%ert98yuasdu

&DFD(*&e

4:57 PM—I don't know what's wrong with my laptop. It just went crazy and then shut down. Kid is drawing in the dirt.

5:39 PM—Still drawing. Lines and circles.

5:55 PM—I'm convinced that Squiggles has absolutely zero super powers. He may also be mentally deficient. He fell asleep in the dirt. I'm going to camp.

Chapter Fifteen

Trent tried to get out of revisiting his super villain subject after the first contact experience, but the professor would hear none of it and sent him off to the mountain to study. He decided to keep his distance.

Monday, June 13th

9:47AM—Arrived at Death Killer's mountain. Couldn't see him anywhere, so I walked around exploring the area. Found crude art work hammered into cliff face. It looks like it is supposed to be a woman. Maybe. It really sucks though.

10:14 AM—Still no sign of Death Killer. I'm glad. I'm keeping my eye on the sky. Meanwhile I'm trying to find out where the villain lives up here. Also, it's been raining. My feet are cold. My hair is wet. My laptop seems to be okay, but it's been rained on, too.

10:33 AM—Death Killer just came out from behind a boulder in a cliffside across the clearing from me. I think it's the door to a hidden cave. Luckily, I wasn't out in the open when he came out. He didn't see me. He took the longest pee I've ever witnessed.

10:52 AM—Villain went flying off ten minutes ago and hasn't come back. I'm going to see if I can get into his cave.

10:53 AM—Nope.

11:33 PM—In jungle at base of mountain. Found Death Killer taking a shower in a waterfall. I think he was singing. His speech bubbles were cloud shaped, and there were musical notes inside them. Sometimes there were several bubbles at once. I'll have to ask about super people singing.

2:19 PM—Witnessed another horrible skinning by freshly showered super villain. Death Killer caught an island panda by freezing its feet to the ground with cold breath. He twisted off its head, peeled off the skin and fur with a quick yank, and flew off back toward the mountain with the skin in one hand and its body in the other.

4:08 PM—I don't know if he ate the panda. There's a fire smoldering near his boulder-door, so maybe he ate. I don't see any carcass. No new bones, either. I wonder if he wasted that whole panda.

4:33 PM—Death Killer almost saw me. I was about to sneak down the mountain when he came bursting out of the ground about twenty feet in front of me. Luckily he was looking the other way, and went flying off. I think I peed again, but my pants are so wet from the jungle, I can't tell.

List of powers discovered today:

> Tunneling
> Freeze Breath
> Super Pee
> Super Singing

Tuesday, June 14th

9:50 AM—Arrival at mountain. No sign of Death Killer.

11:33 AM—Death Killer came outside his cave, gathered something from his fire pit, and went back inside. I haven't seen him in an hour.

12:56 PM—Still no super villain. I'm going to draw.

4:38 PM—Great sketching day. No Death Killer. I wonder what he's doing in there.

5:00 PM—I'm out of here.

Wednesday, June 15th

11:55 AM—Death Killer flew over me on the way to the mountain. He was headed toward the beach. He's been flying low across the sand and scooping up huge handfuls. He's piling something up just out of reach of the surf.

12:58 PM—Clams! It's a big pile of clams. He's having a clambake. He just dug a huge hole by sucking sand into his mouth, and used his laser vision to fuse the sand in the bottom of the hole to steaming glass. Then he flicked his wrist toward the jungle and a whole bush of banana leaves appeared in his hand. He tossed them into the hole and moved the clams on top with a nod.

2:35 PM—Dude ate about sixty pounds of clams. He's expanded to the size of a young walrus. He's lying on the beach.

4:45 PM—Death Killer is gone. I was just looking at him. He was still all big and fat, and just kind of rolling around and then he was gone. I don't know how he did that.

4:47 PM—He reappeared. I think he's asleep, and he accidentally went invisible.

5:05 PM—He farted his walrus weight away. It killed a passing bird, and fish are washing up on the beach. I'm glad to be this far away.

Favorite abilities uncovered today:

  Killer Gas
  Super Scooper
  Mega Mouth
  Translocation
  Expansion
  Invisibility

Thursday, June 16th

9:44 AM— Back at Shark Tooth. I thought I saw a super woman flying around up here, but I can't be sure. Death Killer must still be asleep.

10:59 AM—Villain is outside his cave home—this time I saw behind the boulder when he came out, because he moved it aside—it looks big. He's got a pile of furs from various animals and seems to be sorting through them. I can see the panda.
2:06 PM—Death Killer is gone. I fell asleep.

2:22 PM—He's not gone. He's been working on his "art". I almost walked right into him. If he hadn't been so preoccupied, he would have seen me. He was tapping at the rock super fast, like his fingers were jackhammers. Rock pieces flew all over the place. I still think the relief is supposed to be a woman. Or it might be that panda.

4:09 PM—Death Killer came walking out to the center of the clearing, looked up to the sky, and clapped his hands toward a flock of seagulls above. Birds fell from the air, thumping around his feet. He gathered them up in a pile and waved his hands over them. All their feathers disappeared and the carcasses plumped up roasted. He popped them into his mouth, one after another, feet, heads, giant pocket-bills and all. He ate about twenty. His teeth are scary.

New abilities uncovered today:

71

Death Clap
Microwave Hands
Jack Hammer Fingers
Ant-Art Sensibility

Friday, June 17th

1:34 PM—Saw Death Killer fly over camp this morning, and I followed. He flew over the restricted area, so I stopped. On my way to mountain.

3:53 PM—At the mountain. Death Killer isn't here. His art is coming along. It's not that bad, really.

5:30 PM—Still not home. I wonder what he's up to.

6:13PM—Death Killer is back. He flew down, walked up to his boulder, and then through it into his cave. If I wasn't afraid that I'd snore and he'd hear me, I'd just sleep here. Not looking forward to the hike back.

After a few more days of studying Death Killer, it seems that he has a limitless amount of powers. I've witnessed 45 different ones so far and have no idea where the list will end. I wonder why he lives alone. He must truly be terrible. His powers are useful.

Chapter Sixteen

Trent couldn't find a single spoon that wasn't fused to a fork. He just wanted to eat some oatmeal. He tried avoiding the tines.

The professor sat beside him. He watched Trent try and eat and said, "Super people?"

"I guess so." Trent examined the utensil.

"They can be such monkeys." The professor sipped at a mug of tea. "So, Trent, how are you doing with your work?"

Trent wondered if he should just say everything was fine. He knew that eventually Topper would read his notes, or the end of the study would come and his tremendous shortcomings would be obvious.

He said, "I'm not having such a good time of it, actually, Professor."

Professor Topper sipped his tea. He waited for Trent to explain.

"It's just that I'm not making that much progress. Death Killer is impossible to get close to. He's scary and seems to have unlimited powers. And I don't think the hero kid has any powers at all."

The professor said, "Of course he has powers. You just haven't discovered them yet."

"I don't think I ever will."

"You will. I think you're giving up too easily." He drank tea.

"I don't know. I may not be cut out for this. I'm not even sure why I'm here."

"You're here because you love anthropology and you wanted to experience the Island of Super People. And also

73

because I wanted you here."

Trent let his spork drop into his cooling oatmeal. "Why would you want me here? I'm obviously not good at this. Jen's taking freakin' flying lessons with her subjects. Even Martin's got things going on."

"Oh, he's got things going on, all right." Professor Topper said. "Look, Trent, I have all the faith in the world that you will succeed with these super people. I gave you the hardest assignments on purpose."

"You what?"

The professor smiled. "I see a great anthropologist in you. You have the traits to excel in the field—you're a good listener, you blend in, you have detailed observational skills, you're non-judgmental… The list goes on and on, really."

"But I'm not your best student."

"Do you know that I am one of two scientists in the entire world allowed on this island?"

"I do know that, yes, sir."

"You probably realize, then, that in order to achieve my position, I had to excel in my university studies—that I had to indeed be the best student, get the best grades, et cetera."

Trent shrugged. "Sure."

"That's not how it happened." The professor sipped his tea. "I was an average student as far as grades went. I nearly quit the program when I looked around and saw that there were twenty people in my class doing better at the lessons than I was. Knowing they were my competition in the real world, I was certain I'd never receive funding for any projects or be asked to join a research expedition.

"But one day, on a field study in the wilds of Southwestern North Borneo, my class was about to be murdered by a tutu-obsessed tribe of albino-alligator worshipping maniacs. It was my ability to blend into the background—to fully observe astutely those social beasts around me—that saved me and the rest of my class.

"It's a long story, and I may tell it to you sometime, but just know that it was the qualities beside schoolwork that got my professor's notice. These are the same qualities I see in you—natural abilities to see what's really going on. None of those straight-A students could have even fit into the costume. At any rate—I want you to know that I have the greatest of faith in your abilities."

Trent said, "Really?"

"Really. Now you just keep at it. Use those skills that come so naturally to you. They'll be what get you where you want to be. I promise." The professor stood.

Trent stood, too. He felt like he should shake his teacher's hand. He didn't. He said, "Okay, Professor Topper. I'll keep going."

"I know you will, Trent. And figure out Squiggles' power, would you?" The professor went into his tent.

Trent looked down at the cold oatmeal. He knew if he just left the bowl sitting there, some super person would eat it. Probably Martin's sludge woman. He went to get his equipment together, even stopping to wash the few balloons he'd used.

Chapter Seventeen

Trent sat on a large flat rock above the super boy's favorite mud puddle. He'd thought about what the professor said and used his observational strengths to decide the best place to really communicate with Squiggles. He figured if the kid was relaxed and happy, and in a place where he was used to seeing Trent, that they could have a meaningful exchange of dialogue.

He set up his laptop for note taking.

Saturday, June 18th

11:34AM—Today is the day that I make a breakthrough with Squiggles.

The kid showed up half an hour later and sat in the puddle.

Trent waved and smiled.

The kid ignored him and played in the mud.

12:12PM—Kid is ignoring me. Going to try balloon greeting.

He blew up a balloon and scribbled, *Hi I'm Trent*, on it. He scooted closer to the kid and held the balloon to his face.

Squiggles looked up at him. One of his pinwheel-shaped speech bubbles inflated. **?**

Trent let his balloon deflate. He went back to his laptop.

His notes were garbled. The last one read, 12balloon Kid 12mig ring sito.

"Crap." He blew in the exhaust port and connection outlets, and tapped on its top.

He tried to type.

%^$55di iuo099 da3wq 0#@$^

Trent looked up at the kid. He was watching.

"Come on," he said. He tapped at the machine.

A chat window opened. A message said, *Hi, Trent!*

He ignored it and blew on the laptop. Squiggles was watching him, so at least he had his attention. But he wanted to be ready to write down methods he was using to communicate. Longhand made it more difficult with ballooning. He tapped at the screen.

There was a chirping sound and another message appeared, *Hi, Trent!*

He suddenly wondered who could be instant-messaging him. They had no internet service. *Who could set up a network on the island?*

Trent answered. *Jen?*

No.

Martin?

No.

Who is this?

Squiggles.

Trent looked up. The kid was staring straight at him, smiling wide.

"What?" Trent looked at the kid.

He sat in the mud smiling.

Trent blew up a balloon, wrote on it, and held it up. *Are you doing this?*

Squiggles answered with a whirly speech bubble, *?*

The student looked at the boy in the mud. He typed in the IM, *Are you doing this?* He looked up at Squiggles.

The kid smiled and nodded.

On Trent's screen, the IM chirped again. Trent realized that the chatboxes looked like speech bubbles. The super boy's chat bubble looked like the weird pinwheels he used to speak.

The bubble read, *I am not boring.*

Trent typed, *What?*

I've read your text. You think I'm boring.

A journal entry appeared on Trent's screen. It began with how boring the kid was.

Is this really you?

It's really me. The boy nodded.

Trent sat and looked at him for a moment. He saw his tentative smile, his electric eyes, and the fine lines that ran across his bald head. He noticed his nose, and details in his chest emblem.

He typed, *I'm sorry for saying you were boring.*

It's okay.

So, your name is really Squiggles?

No. Everyone calls me Captain Fuckup. I like Squiggles better.

Why do they call you Captain Fuckup?

I don't have any powers.

Trent looked over at the boy. He wanted to jump up and hug the muddy little guy.

Are you kidding? He typed. *If you can speak to me through my computer, you've got a power! THIS is a power!*

Really? All I'm doing is talking.

No one else can talk to me like this.

The kid shrugged. *Well, talking isn't a super power. But it's nice to do it anyway. I'm happy someone can actually hear me. You are the first person I've ever talked to.*

Trent looked at the little boy. He smiled with him, letting the moment seal its golden realizations. Then he typed.

The two of them sat and talked on Trent's laptop until its battery ran down and Trent noticed that the sky was darkening. He promised Squiggles that he would talk with him again soon.

He returned to camp happier than he'd been since he'd arrived. And hopeful—ridiculously, over-confidently hopeful.

Chapter Eighteen

Death Killer was arranging boulders.

Trent used the previous day's success to propel him toward his goal of connecting with the villain and thoroughly completing his assignments—doing a good job and maybe even making Topper proud. The breakthrough with Squiggles took up most of his thoughts, but there was still a great deal of fear for his life poking through that confidence. Death Killer was a completely different situation than the super boy.

The student stood behind his favorite hiding place in the rocks, psyching himself up. "Okay, Trent. You can do this. He could have killed you and he didn't."

Trent slunk from behind the boulders and walked carefully toward the villain.

Death Killer stacked huge stones into a pyramid. Fire shot from a few of the horns on his head.

Trent dropped behind another big rock. He thought about being flattened by a boulder or burned by horn-flames. Visions of the giant Death Killer and foot-prison flashed through his head. Then the story of the professor saving his class from the tribe of dangerous weirdos came to mind. Trent got up and walked toward the villain.

He paused at a clump of palm trees. Trent whispered to himself, "It's okay. You can do this. Think of the professor. Think of the ocean, or boobs, or margaritas on the beach…" He ducked around the trees.

Death Killer paused and turned his head slightly.

Trent stopped walking.

The villain looked at the huge rock in his hands. He

flipped it over, appraising it.

Trent stood motionless.

Death Killer grunted, and tossed the boulder backward over Trent's head and off the distant side of the mountain. The super man went back to arranging boulders, picking a new one from the bunch at his feet.

Trent breathed. He chanted a no-pee mantra in his head and started slowly forward.

The villain put a rock on his growing pyramid and glared over his shoulder at the approaching student.

Trent froze.

When Death Killer went back to work, Trent took a few more steps toward him. Trent could see the jagged edges of the bony spines on the super villain's back. Wisps of black smoke drifted around his super skull. The bands of color that ran along his shoulders, arms, back, and legs were bright in the sun. His overblown muscles stretched and bunched like they were their own separate monsters.

Trent walked up beside the super man, forcing himself to meet Death Killer's eyes when he turned and gazed down.

The super villain didn't glare or sneer. But there was no smile or welcome in his eyes, either. A tiny flicker of flame escaped a horn, but nothing overly frightening. Death Killer stood with a boulder in hand, looking down with a blank expression.

Trent didn't break eye contact. He fumbled for a balloon and marker in his pocket. He let sweat pour down his head, blinking it away with half a nervous smile. He blew up the balloon sloppily, looking around it at the passive super villain.

He looked down only to quickly scribble a greeting and held up the balloon.

Hi, my name is Tret.

Death Killer dropped the rock. It bounced into his knee—which he didn't seem to notice—and onto the pile. The villain held up his left hand, and talons shot out of the ends of the fingers of his gloves like little switchblades. Without an expression, he flicked the balloon with a long, pointed nail. It popped.

Trent jumped. He looked up at the villain. He shakily pulled out another balloon, wrote the same thing on it, and held it up.

The super villain popped that one, too.

He blew up another and wrote, *My name is Trent. Nice to meet you.*

Death Killer stone-facedly denied him. He popped the balloon.

Trent wrote something different on the fourth balloon. *Stop popping my bubbles!*

Death Killer's eyes flashed red under his thick mask. He reached out and snatched a handful of Trent's shirt. With a snarl—showing two rows of needle teeth—the super villain leapt into the air and flew over the side of the mountain with Trent dangling by his claws.

They plunged down the jagged face of Shark Tooth Mountain.

Trent screamed. He held the villain's hand with both of his. Lumpy spires of black lava rock rushed under them. The jagged cliff-side was a blur. Trent screamed more.

The villain dove straight down to the sea, pulling up at the last second, and dunking Trent into the briny waves. He took the student on a terrible ride around the island, dipping him over and over into the sea like a squealing tea bag.

Death Killer swooped out of the sky and set Trent in the middle of his camp. He put him down in front of the dinner table—where Martin, Jen and Natalie were eating. The villain flew away.

Trent stood there dripping, facing the table. He held the, *Stop popping my bubbles!* balloon in his hand.

Martin said, "How's it going with Death Killer?"

Trent let tears mix with the saltwater dripping from his hair. He shook and quivered from his lips to his knees. The balloon slipped from his fingers. He opened his mouth, but couldn't say a word, so he closed it.

Chapter Nineteen

I have something to show you.
  What is it?
  It's a surprise.
Trent followed Squiggles through the jungle, balancing his laptop with one hand and typing with the other while watching out for obstacles on the path.
  Come on. Just tell me where we're going.
  You'll see.
He did see. Trent realized that Squiggles was leading him into the restricted area along the same path he'd seen him take many times before.
  Trent typed, *Squiggles, we can't go in there. It's dangerous. It's restricted. We could die.*
  There's nothing dangerous.
  Yes, there is. Stop.
  You're funny, Trent.
Squiggles kept walking. He picked up the pace.
Trent stopped.
The boy kept going.
  Squiggles! Stop!
He kept walking down the path. No speech bubble IM appeared.
  Squiggles!
Trent couldn't see the kid anymore. He wondered what to do. He'd stood in the same place many other times and the solution had always been to turn around and go back to camp. But this time he couldn't do that. He had to convince Squiggles to stay the hell out of there. Super or not, radiation could do serious damage to a growing boy.

Despite his own fear of exposure, Trent hurried down the path behind the little hero.

He closed his laptop to make better time and jogged along the path, crossing a stream and running up a slight hill. He came around a corner and the path widened.

Squiggles stood there waiting for him, a big smile on his face.

Trent flipped open his computer to talk to the boy, but slapped it shut as the jungle erupted around them.

The tops of the trees waved and bent. There was a whirring, hissing sound followed by the crack of an explosion above their heads. Smoke darkened the air. Trent dove for the ground. Huge things dropped from the canopy above. Metal clanged, wood creaked and popped, the ground vibrated.

A rock jammed into Trent's side as he fell. His laptop flew into a bush. Branches, leaves, and clods of earth pelted him. He got up to run and met the barrels of several guns pointed at his face.

A voice shouted, "We have a positive, sir!"

Trent froze. There were several soldiers aiming rifles at him. Over their heads loomed a cyber-trooper, its multiple eye-lenses whirring under its black faceplate as it focused on layers of jungle around them. It stomped backward, ripping trees down and trampling jungle debris to compost.

A soldier pulled Squiggles up from under a fallen tree. He hoisted the boy off the ground and said, "Aw, shit, sir. It's only the little retard."

A deep voice spoke up right behind Trent. "At ease, soldiers. This here's a scientist."

The soldiers let the barrels of their guns drop. They backed up.

"Let the kid go," the deep voice said.

When the soldier let go of Squiggles, the boy ran to Trent and plastered himself to his hip. The deep-voiced man stepped from behind Trent and grabbed Squiggles by the shoulder, prying him off.

He tossed Squiggles onto the path and said, "Go home, capeback!" He kicked at the little hero.

The boy looked to Trent.

A cyber-trooper stomped between them and with a whir and click of its gears, aimed its weapons at the boy.

The cyber-trooper raised his massive gun-fist and shot one ear-ripping round over the boy's head.

Squiggles ducked. He ran down the path.

The man with the deep voice grabbed Trent by his shirt and spun him around.

"You were warned that this area is restricted." He tossed Trent to the ground.

A cyber-trooper stomped backward, shaking the path.

Two soldiers pinned Trent to the ground and rolled him over. His mouth was open when they rolled him, and his teeth dug into the dirt of the path. He tasted mud, and shit, and rot. He hoped he wasn't eating radiation.

The soldiers cuffed his hands and pulled him to his feet. Trent spit dirt. Mud drooled down his chin. The man loomed above him as the soldier held him up.

"I'm Lieutenant Rockwood. I want to know why you're here, where you know you're not supposed to be."

Trent tried to talk but fear and dirt-throat stopped him. He coughed and spit mud. He finally croaked, "Following that kid."

The lieutenant laughed a hollow laugh and said, "You're following around the retard of the capebacks?"

His soldiers snickered.

Rockwood smiled. "All right, let's get this fuckin' scientist out of here."

They pushed Trent along the path.

The soldiers roughly escorted Trent back to his camp. They shoved him past Martin to Professor Topper's tent and explained where they'd found him. Rockwood harassed the professor and told the gathering anthropologists to stay out of the restricted areas, or they'd be kicked off the island.

The Professor told Trent, "I'm surprised and disappointed in you. Colonel Shank was quite clear with us about not entering that area. You're jeopardizing this entire study. You'll be lucky if you leave camp for a month."

Trent hung his head.

The soldiers removed the cuffs.

Lieutenant Rockwood told the professor, "Well, Topper. It seems you've got this under control. But this is your one chance. If any of the rest of your group sets foot into restricted space, you're all off the island for good."

"I understand," said the professor, glaring at Trent.

"Good, then." The soldier looked down at Trent and then made a motion with his hand. The cyber-troopers at the edge of camp perked up and the squad of soldiers moved out.

Trent watched Rockwood looking back at him until he was out of sight.

Then he risked eye contact with the professor.

Topper was grinning at him like an idiot. "Great job, my boy! Those monsters have no right to be here, tossing their boundaries willy-nilly. Threatening us with expulsion. And you stood right up to them. You followed your subject in the name of science in a purely scientific manner with steadfast determination and consequences be damned just like a real scientist does."

"Uh," Trent said.

"That's right, Trent. You keep it up. Good job."

"Uh, okay. I will."

"You will, Trent. You will. And great job with Squiggles, by the way. I knew you'd figure that out. And, happily, those soldiers returned your laptop. See you at dinner."

Trent fell into his tent and passed out.

Chapter Twenty

"I wish you'd just have let me nap." Trent said.

"You're always sleepin'. Besides, you need something to cheer you up and relax you after what happened to you this morning." Martin said.

Trent asked, "How is this going to relax me?"

Martin gaped at him. The crowd behind him swayed—all blue, white and red. "Are you serious? Mud wrestling with hot super chicks? What's more relaxing than this?" He gestured at the spectacle around them.

They stood in a natural hollow in the jungle about a mile from Hero Village—a deep indentation in the forest that had been cleared of trees. Log benches and stump chairs were set up around the cleared circle. There were heroes gathered on them in groups, waiting for the event. Excited speech bubbles burst and popped all around. They were eating meat on sticks, and passing around cups of something yellow that puckered their lips when they drank.

Trent didn't see mud. On either side of the arena were low huts like the homes in the village. There was movement inside the huts, but the doors were closed. It was impossible to see more than shadow and light behind the fronds.

Martin surveyed the scene obviously hunting for something in particular. He led Trent to a bench. "Okay, just stay here. Miss Sunshine is supposed to be here, and I don't see her, so…"

"Why am I here, Martin?"

The frat boy kept scanning the scene. "Huh?"

"You're here to find that heroine you follow around. You don't need me for that. Why did you bring me?"

Martin looked at him. "Because you need some action, man. Now sit back and enjoy the show. I'm gonna go find my girl."

"I'm going with you."

Trent followed Martin, scanning the crowd. He was also hoping to find Squiggles. He hadn't heard from him since that morning in the jungle.

Speech bubbles suddenly burst throughout the mingling super people and they started taking seats.

Madame Manifestor stood between the huts, in the dirt circle.

She spoke, and Trent happened to be where he could read it, *Welcome to The Challenge!* Heroes clapped around the circle. Trent clapped, too. He turned back to find Martin slipping through the crowd. He followed him.

There was another speech bubble floating beside the leader. *We have some nasty villains to take care of. Heroes! Calling heroes!*

The spider woman shot twin webs from her spinnerets into the sky. She jumped into the air and disappeared.

A super woman burst from each of the huts the moment their leader vanished.

Jagged shouting bubbles flashed and popped among the crowd. Super people clapped excitedly and exchanged quick speech bubbles.

Trent poked his head between super people at the edge of the circle. He looked for Miss Sunshine, but was distracted by the show.

One of the heroes—a black-haired woman in a blue and red bikini with white boots and a blue cape with white stars—was wearing a green mask. *Green?* The other super woman wore a red suit with white shoulders and blue boots. She had no cape.

The red-suited heroine faced Trent and he read her jagged bubble. *Villain! I shall vanquish thee!*

The green-masked "villain" stepped forward and grabbed the hero woman by both arms. Green Mask picked her up and slammed her feet-first into the rocky dirt. The red-suited hero was driven into the ground like a drill. Jagged bubbles popped around both of their heads. The bikinied super woman looked around at the audience through her green mask.

Trent realized he'd lost Martin. He walked through the crowd around the ring. No Miss Sunshine. And now no Martin. He watched the fight.

The heroine unleashed heat vision, tearing into Green Mask's bare midriff and throwing her backward. The woman in the red suit opened her mouth wide. Blue light poured out and struck the other super woman in her green mask.

Green Mask spun around and pulled her cape up over her head. She vanished and reappeared behind the bewildered heroine. The cape came up again, this time over both of the super women and both of them disappeared.

"Holy shit!" Trent yelled. He gaped at the heroes around him cheering with harsh bubbles.

The circle remained empty for nearly one minute.

Then bikini woman blinked in. Her hair was frosty, and the green mask hung half-off her face. She was panting, but smiling. There was a huge hunk of blonde hair in her hand.

The audience cheered—clapping and shouting big, excited bubbles.

The other heroine flashed in behind the green-masked one. She lay on the ground, writhing in pain. Madame Manifestor appeared and declared Green Mask the winner. Other women helped the injured heroine to one of the huts.

Martin approached Trent as the hero woman ducked into one of the huts in the center. "I can't find Miss Sunshine. She was supposed to fight tonight, but she's not here."

A new fight began in the center.

"What is this, Martin?"

The frat boy watched two hero women square off over Trent's head. "Wha? Oh. It's training. One plays the villain. See?" He pointed.

One of the women had a black cape that was obviously not part of her body.

The cape was being burned off. The super woman grew twice her size, the cape falling behind her and smoldering.

As a giant, she snatched up the other super woman in her fat hand and squeezed. The heroine erupted in jagged bubbles. Trent read the last one. It said, *Help!*

Her face turned red, then blue. The giantess squeezed and squeezed. Trent could hear bones snapping under the thick finger pads. The tiny heroine jinked and jolted in the other's grip. Blood shot from her nose and mouth. She fell limp.

The crowd went wild.

Trent was horrified. He turned to Martin. "This is sick!"

Martin said, "This is the super hero life." He went back to watching bystanders dragging the limp super woman out of the circle.

They laid her down and a super man bent over her and blew some sparkly silver stuff into her nose and mouth. She kicked and sat up fast, gasping. A jagged bubble shot above her. *Gah!*

The super man wiped blood from the injured super woman's face. The other heroine had returned to normal size.

"The villains are stronger," Trent observed.

Martin spoke without turning, his eyes were on the next set of warriors, "No shit. It's training."

Trent left. Martin didn't notice.

On the way back to camp, Trent thought about how to tell the professor about what he'd just seen. He wondered if the professor had ever attended an event like that. He thought he must have.

Trent replayed the last battle in his mind. He saw that squished heroine—the blood pouring from her nose and mouth. He was happy she was alive.

The student ambled along through the jungle, thinking about Martin, and the super heroes. He decided to draw.

Trent found a small waterfall with plenty of large rocks

below it. He sat on a flat boulder, pulled out his notebook, and began drawing the super woman being squished. He'd really hated that.

The sound of the water soothed Trent, and soon he was involved in sketching. The stress in his body eased. He sat there beside the waterfall for an hour or so, lost in drawing. "This is better."

As Trent walked back to camp, he thought about Squiggles and wondered what the kid had been up to.

A brown-orange blur rushed from the jungle in front of him. There was an ear-screwing scream, and Trent was knocked backward onto the ground in front of a thick tree, snapping off a lower branch with his body.

A shaggy thing with yellow curved teeth and leather skin gnashed at him. Spit flew through the air. The creature hissed and gurgled. It smelled like pee on rotten fur. Its foamy jaws snapped, and Trent barely had time to instinctively put his hands up and push into the beast's greasy neck.

Trent cowered below an island boar—a monster nearly the size of a bear with tusks and hooves and a hunger for anything warm and bloody. A sharp hoof dug into his left calf. With a fiery shriek of inflamed adrenaline, Trent kicked with both feet and shoved the grunting thing away. He scrambled backward, pushing against the tree to stand.

The boar huffed and lowered its foamy snout. It raked the ground up with a hoof and prepared to charge. Trent jumped up and barely caught a thick limb. He pulled himself up as the wild pig ran at him.

The boar crashed into the tree. Trent clamored up the branch.

"Fuck you!" he screamed, spitting and starting to cry. "Fuck you!"

He pulled himself up, reaching for the next limb above him.

The pig shook itself off and squealed. It raised on its hind legs, standing nearly eight feet tall, sniffing and slobbering right under Trent. It jumped at Trent's feet, pushing at his left boot with its snout.

Trent screamed and jumped to catch the next limb. The limb he stood on snapped, dumping Trent right on top of the pig.

The angry animal shook the student off and bounded onto the trail, snarling and squealing.

Piss flew from the beast as it twisted free, spraying Trent. He wretched, and clawed his way out from under the broken branch. His left leg dragged. It hurt, and putting weight on it hurt worse. Trent staggered backward to the tree, huffing and yelling whatever words came to his thick, dry tongue.

"Shit fucking pig! Ass fuck! Ham-hock bacon shit ass!"

The boar shrieked and raised onto its hind legs, pawing the air like a murderous stallion. It crashed down with a grunt, ripping at the jungle floor with razor hooves. The boar geared up to charge again.

Trent rocked side to side, wondering where to dodge. The creature's yellow eyes drove into his brain. His ribs felt like they'd been broken off into his lungs. His leg burned and threatened to collapse when he put weight on it. His right eye was swollen shut. He couldn't catch his breath. The shaggy monster was coming to eat him. Trent saw a tiny leaf stuck on the end of one of the pig's tusks. He focused on it, shining in a patch of sun.

The beast charged.

Foam flew from its open mouth. Its piston-legs drove it thumping toward him. At the last moment, Trent found his voice and will. He shrieked and threw his arms over his face. Hooves beat the ground.

There was a tearing sound and the hooves stuttered. Trent opened his eyes to see the boar's headless body tumbling toward him. He managed to dive.

The thing whumped into the tree. Blood sploshed over Trent in a gory wave.

Trent jumped to his feet.

Death Killer floated in front of him, holding the boar's head in one clawed hand. He smiled and drifted over to the twitching monster beside Trent.

"Holy fuck!" Trent stomped his feet in a circle. He flung

blood from his hands.

Grabbing the headless boar by its severed spine, the villain yanked the hide free of its body in one pull. Bloody purple flesh tumbled to the ground and more blood sloshed out, drenching Trent's feet.

Death Killer turned in the air to look down at the shivering student.

Then he flew off with the head and hide of the thing that nearly ate Trent.

Trent limped into camp and collapsed. The professor logged the incident and lectured the students as Natalie cleaned Trent's wounds and bandaged his leg. He told Trent to take the next day or two off, and talked about perhaps implementing a buddy system. Trent hoped that if that happened, he'd be teamed up with Jen. Or Natalie.

Chapter Twenty-One

So is it really that fun to poke dead stuff all the time?
Yes.

Trent looked up and smiled. Squiggles stood poking washed-up jellyfish.

Come on, let's go to the tide pools.

How is your leg? Squiggles asked.

Better, thank you. It could use some stretching. Let's go.

The boy stopped poking and followed Trent down the beach.

Martin was there. "Hey, Trent," he said, looking up from his hand-held, solar-powered video game.

"Hey, Martin. How ya doin'?"

"Damnit!" He pounded his game in his fist. "I'm fine. Or I was."

"Why, what's up?"

"*Zombie Bloodbath* just went all screwy."

Trent glanced over at Squiggles. "What's up with it?"

Martin showed him. The screen was snowy. Sometimes the picture would clear and Trent thought he saw an avatar that looked a lot like Squiggles.

"When did it start doing that?" Trent asked.

"Huh? Oh, just now." He hit the game to his palm.

Trent typed on his laptop, *Are you doing that on purpose?*
Doing what?
Making his video game messed up.

The boy looked at Trent. *No.*

Can you put your image on his screen?
What?
Just concentrate on his machine. Put an image of you in

93

it. Display that on the screen.

"What the hell?" Martin asked. He flipped his game so Trent could see.

Squiggles was on his screen. The little guy was running around shooting zombies and collecting ammo.

"How's your little creeper doin' it, Trent?"

"What?"

"Captain Fuckup. How'd he get in my game?"

Trent looked over at the boy. He was poking a starfish with a stick. "His name is Squiggles."

"Whatever." Martin shot zombies with the little hero's avatar. "How's he doing this?"

"I don't know."

Have you done this before?

No. It's not hard, though. I like it.

Trent thought for a moment. He got up and motioned for Squiggles.

"Where ya goin'?" Martin asked.

"Camp," Trent said. He typed, *Let's go see what else you can do.*

Squiggles followed. So did Martin.

Trent gathered electronics. He put his phone and GPS on the table.

He said, "Martin, I need some electronics."

"Looks like you've got plenty." He moved his game into the sun.

"Not as cool as yours. Come on, whatever you've got."

"Okay, but I want your little friend there to be in my game again. He was kickin' ass."

They collected a radio, two GPS locators, a portable DVD player, a laptop, the hand-held game, two mp3 players, and two digital cameras.

Squiggles stood in front of the electronics on the table. Lights flashed and things beeped. The cameras went off.

Trent typed, *I think you affect electronics. Pick up one of those things from the table.*

The boy picked up a digital camera. The flash went off like a strobe light. He put it down. The GPS locators started whistling, each a different tone. The radio came on, and began flipping through stations. Porn flashed on the DVD player's screen.

Martin put his game down and his hands to his ears. "Stop, already!"

The video game repeated what he said in a high-pitched tinny voice, *Stop already! Stop! Stop! Stop already!*

Squiggles put his hand over the pile of stuff on the table. Everything turned on and made noise or lit up. He moved his hand away and the electronics quieted. He moved his hand over them. They went nuts.

You control electronics.

What are electronics?

Trent started laughing.

Squiggles spoke in bubble, *?*

We need to explore your powers. This is amazing. You can make machines work. At least the ones with circuitry.

I don't want to make machines work with circuitry.

No, I mean... It's hard to explain. It's a great thing. It means you can control machines with an electrical charge. We should explore it more. But not right now. What do you think?

I like to explore.

Martin said, "None of my stuff had better be messed up. 'Bout all I've got is video games and porn DVDs, since Miss Sunshine's gone."

"You never hooked up with your super lady?"

"She didn't show up. I haven't seen her at all."

Trent smiled. "Maybe she's avoiding you."

Martin scowled and beat the side of his video game into his palm.

Chapter Twenty-Two

Death Killer picked up another bone from the pile. He held it up and turned it over, trying it in different places before he finally found where he wanted it and fused the vertebrae to the rest of the sculpture.

Trent sat behind a rock, not far away. He thought the villain probably knew he was there.

The super man was working on a delicate bone sculpture. He'd been at it since Trent showed up at the mountain.

As he rummaged for another bone in the pile, a group of super people from Hero Village appeared. Two just blinked in, one popped up from the ground, and six more came from out of the sky.

The heroes surrounded Death Killer. He stood, leaving the femur he'd chosen for his art in the pile. The villain sized-up his visitors.

Trent kept behind the rock, but poked his head out enough to see what was going on. He read what a large hero made of shining black obsidian was saying. His big, angry bubble read, *We know you have something to do with Elixir disappearing.*

Death Killer's jagged bubble was facing away from Trent, so he couldn't read his reply. But judging from the reaction of the heroes, it was nothing they wanted to hear. Trent moved closer, sneaking behind a clump of trees.

He heard something behind him. Natalie ran toward him, crouched over.

Trent waved her back. She scuffled over to the trees.

"What are you doing here?" he hissed.

Natalie whispered, "I saw them talking about coming

96

here. I came to warn you."

"This looks dangerous."

"Agreed."

They watched through the trees.

A hero with a weird lumpy head that looked like hairy broccoli said, *We will have no more of your lies!*

The obsidian hero punched at the villain.

Death Killer caught the hero's glass-knife arm, snapped it off, and stabbed it into his chest.

The hero shrieked.

"This is awful," Natalie said.

A short, fat super man beside the injured hero turned white hot and bounced toward Death Killer. The villain caught him. He took the fat man by the ankle and swung him at the tall broccoli-headed guy, knocking their heads together.

The fat guy's thick skull crunched into the cheek and jaw of the tall bumpy-headed hero. Bones broke in a hard, wet thwacks. There was a sizzling sound and a puff of smoke. The tall one fell backward, and Death Killer caught him by the cape. He pulled, and ripped the blue skin right off the broccoli hero's back. The super man screamed, spinning through air. Blood shot from his torn neck like a sprinkler, spraying the other heroes and soaking the ground. The villain tossed the cape.

"Oh my God!" Natalie yelled.

Death Killer spun in a circle, holding the fat hero's booted leg in a bone-snapping grip. He whipped him around and around. Blood pooled in his white hot eyes. The villain swung the heated super man into another hero and let him go, sending both of them crashing into the cliffside. There was a blast of fire, and rocks tumbled down on the heroes.

Pieces bounced off the ground beside Trent and Natalie, thocking off a tree. "Get down," Trent told her. "You need to get out of here."

"Me? *You* need to get out of here. Come on!"

"I can't. I have to observe."

"I'm telling you to get out of here. I'm the TA. That

counts. Let's go."

"Look," Trent said, pointing.

Death Killer batted away a photon bolt, and sent a burst of lasers from his eyes back at the hero that threw it. His beams connected, searing the hero's eyes shut in a smoking, popping, screaming second. The hero staggered backward, his hands producing wild balls of lightning that he began hurling haphazardly. He blinked out.

Broccoli hero staggered near their trees. A thick speech bubble filled with garbled letters slid from his mouth and popped. The super man fell to his knees in the dirt, just in front of their hiding place. His eyes rolled into his head and he passed out. Blood pumped from the tear where his cape had been.

Trent watched the fight, putting a hand out for Natalie to hold. She took it.

"We need to get out of here, Trent." She pushed her glasses up.

Obsidian man was back on his feet. He sliced at Death Killer with his remaining arm. The villain jumped into the air and burned into the glassy hero's blue-suited chest with eye-lasers, melting grooves into his flesh. The obsidian man shrieked a jagged bubble as his body melted and parted at its new bubbly seams—*Aaaargh!* He staggered backward and fell.

Another hero attacked—a whirling ball of red, white and blue needles spun just under the villain. Death Killer flicked at the spiky ball and sent it flying. It crashed straight into the trees in front of the students. A pretty heroine fell to the ground. She stood up, retracted her spines, and launched herself in a flying corkscrew at Death Killer.

The bone sculpture teetered and clattered as she flew past.

"Run, Natalie. I'll be fine. Just get back to camp, I'll meet you there." He squeezed her hand and let it go.

"Both of us, Trent. Come. On!" She ran toward the path.

Trent watched her go and then made for a nearby boulder, tripping over Broccoli Man, who was crawling away sobbing. He got up and found himself in the middle of the worst of it. Fire, ice, and super heroes fell around him. He nearly lost his head to a photon bolt. Trent ran for what seemed to be a break in the battle and skidded behind a short, wide boulder.

Death Killer had the needle girl by both arms. He slammed her straight into the ground, face-first.

Yelp! She fell into a loose heap.

The villain kicked her head, spinning her over the side of the mountain.

Natalie yelled for Trent from the distance, but he saw that she was headed down the mountain. He turned back to the action.

A basketball-sized rock flew across the clearing and smashed into the cliffside—shattering and raining big chunks of stone and dirt. A rock hit the corner of Death Killer's sculpture. It popped the sculpture off its wooden stand. The delicate art slowly rolled through the smoky air. Without thinking, Trent leapt over the low boulder and caught the sculpture as it fell straight into his hands.

Balls of fire erupted in a line, starting in the clearing and working their way toward Trent.

"Shit!" He yelled, holding the sculpture as gingerly as possible while running away from the fight. A blast of ice shot past his head as he ran toward a new hiding place.

Death Killer spun in a circle, lasering, microwaving, and freezing alternately. His claws were open knives, his horns erupted with spraying plasma—a wide stream of it hit the bikini woman from the training demonstration, blasting off her foot and melting most of her left leg. Burning flesh, like drops of flaming plastic, peppered the ground behind her. She flew away smoking with a long jagged scream bubble trailing behind her, *AAAAaaaaaaa-aaa-aa-aaaa!*

Trent ducked behind a rock as melted slag rained around him. When he looked up again, two more heroes tumbled away from the fight, one of them missing an arm.

Death Killer swung the red and white arm at another who spit balls of fire. He threw the severed limb like a spear, jamming it fingers-first into the fire shooter's mouth.

Gack! the hero choked.

The villain leapt on him, shoving the arm further down his fire-breathing throat. He pried the hero's mouth open, mashing and pushing. Death Killer pulled the super man's lower jaw down—snapping the gagging hero's jawbone from his skull. Fire burst from around the arm in the super man's mouth.

The villain pushed the arm down into the hero's esophagus and tossed him and his bloody jaw off the mountain.

"Holy fuck," Trent whispered.

A boulder smashed into Death Killer, driving him into the blackened mess that had been his art studio.

Death Killer rose from the dusty rubble and spit bullets of the broken boulder back at the woman who'd tossed it. She caught the first ten or fifteen, but the villain kept spitting and advancing on her. Rocks flew into her face and body, leaving craters in her shining red suit, and opening blood and bone geysers in her beautiful super face.

Uhn! Ooof! Aaaiiieeeee!

Her left eye was punctured and torn out along with the bridge of her nose. A jagged rock with bits of eyeball and bloody cartilage bounced to a stop beside Trent's hand. The super woman fell backward, her bloody white cape fluttering around her. Death Killer jumped on top of her before her cape settled to the dusty ground.

The villain pounded his fist into her face, breaking bones in a sick crunch, and driving her head into the ground. Her legs twitched under him. Death Killer stood and jumped on the fallen woman's chest, stomping his foot into her ribs, snapping them loudly. She vanished before he could do it again.

The super villain whipped around and found no further attackers. The remaining heroes had fled. He surveyed the scene. Dust settled. Rocks slid down the mountainside. Fires smoldered.

Death Killer shuffled toward the place where he'd been working on the sculpture. He found a divot in the ground—

black and melted. Charred, smashed bones lay fused into vulcanized stone.

The villain kicked the ground. A jagged bubble flew from his lips *SCULPTURE!*

Trent crawled out from behind the rock. He held the fragile sculpture out for the villain to see.

Death Killer didn't notice him at first. Trent had to walk up to the seething super man.

When the villain did see the unmasked one approaching with his bone art, he snatched it and stalked a few feet away.

Death Killer examined his sculpture, turning it over, checking the seams. He glanced up suspiciously at the student. Trent stood and tried not to shake. Death Killer put the sculpture on the ground and walked around it. He looked at Trent.

The villain was genuinely surprised and happy that his art was safe.

Trent met the super man's eyes. They weren't glowing red anymore.

A smooth, round speech bubble slipped from Death Killer's mouth. *Thank you.*

"Thank you?" Trent said it out loud. He searched his pockets for balloons and marker. When he found them, he blew up a balloon and wrote, *You're welcome.* He held it up. "Thank you?"

Death Killer smiled at Trent. Razor teeth shone in the sun.

The villain picked up his sculpture and started walking toward his cave. He looked over his shoulder at Trent standing there on the glassy ground, gaping at him. Death Killer motioned for the student to follow him.

Trent blew up a balloon at the entrance to Death Killer's cave. It said, *Why did they attack you?*

A jagged bubble answered, *BASTARDS.*

Trent nodded.

The villain tinkered with his art.

Trent blew up another balloon. *I really like that sculpture.*

Death Killer looked at Trent. He answered in a jagged

bubble. *YOU DO?*

Trent smiled. *Yes.* He sat down and pulled out some balloons.

REALLY?

Yes. It's a balanced piece. Very interesting. Aesthetically pleasing. Trent could barely believe he was speaking with Death Killer. He thought about the battle that had only just ended. There was blood on the villain. There were still pieces of heroes scattered about the clearing. A bush smoldered.

The super man asked, *YOU THINK SO?*

Yes. I like it.

NO ONE'S EVER SEEN MY ART.

Trent watched Death Killer's face soften. *I'd like to see it finished.*

The villain looked at him for a moment. He nodded and bent to pick a bone from the pile beside his front door.

Death Killer went back to work on his sculpture.

Trent spent the rest of the day watching. The super man even let him hand over a few bones.

Chapter Twenty-Three

Trent jumped when a hand landed on his shoulder. He nearly choked on soup.

The professor sat down beside him at the table. "Sorry, did I startle you?"

Trent nodded. "I guess I'm a little jumpy."

Professor Topper laughed harshly. "I think we all are."

"So, Trent, it seems things are going good for you. What's been happening with your research?"

Trent slurped soup. "I've been hanging out with Death Killer every day for the past few days to watch him work on his art. Sometimes he lets me hand him supplies. And he talks to me. He hasn't dumped me in the ocean or burned off my clothes."

The professor laughed. "Good to hear, Trent. Good to hear. And how about your little hero?"

"Squiggles? I've made even more progress with him. Now that we can communicate, I've been helping him develop his powers."

"Oh? Tell me about his powers." Professor Topper set down a steaming pan of potato soup and scooped out a bowl for himself.

"He has power over electronics."

"Over what?"

Trent smiled. "Electronics. So far everything with circuitry that I've presented, he can affect."

The professor sat looking at Trent. "Electronics?"

"Yep."

"That's very interesting."

"I thought so, too." Trent got another bowl of soup.

The professor said, "It's the first I've ever heard of an islander being born with that power. It's not a power one would expect super people to evolve on an island inhabited with people who lack the concept of electricity or complex machinery."

"I agree. It's why no other super people recognize the power. It's why they call him Captain Fuckup."

"Indeed." Professor Topper put his hand on his chin and thought. "At any rate, kudos for the discovery. I'm very proud of you."

"Thank you, Professor."

"Thanks for what?" Martin asked, plopping down beside Trent.

"Oh, uh. Nothing," Trent said.

Jen sat across the table from Trent, beside the professor. She sighed.

"What's going on, Jen?" The professor asked.

Jen looked up with tears in her eyes. "I can't find Fabulous Man. I haven't seen him for days. No one has."

Professor Topper said, "What do you mean, no one has?"

"I asked around. No one's seen him. Some heroes are worried. They say that heroes go missing sometimes. More lately."

Trent said, "I've been hearing about missing people quite a bit, too."

"Actually, I've heard of disappearances lately as well. There has been some rumbling among the heroes about it." The professor said.

Martin said, "Welcome to the club. I haven't been able to find my sweet little hottie, Miss Sunshine, either." He slurped some soup.

"Well, this is indeed something that bears investigation." The professor stood and called Natalie. To the students he said, "You see what you can find out, but be discreet. I'm going to speak to the leaders of the tribes and see if I can't get to the bottom of this." He ducked into his tent as Natalie came out of it. She followed him right back in.

The students shrugged and finished their dinner.

Chapter Twenty-Four

Trent was writing notes about Death Killer's latest artistic endeavor when Squiggle-chat opened.

I want to show you something.

What?

It's a secret.

I'm not going to the restricted area.

No messages came for a while. Trent grinned and went back to typing.

I'll bring something to show you.

Trent laughed. *Okay. Bring it to camp.*

On my way.

Squiggles showed up with a very strange object. He handed it to Trent.

It was a flat, glass and metal rectangle about the size of a cell phone. There were raised buttons on it—a big yellow knob and a small red push-button. The surface was etched with a representation of a circuit board. It was warm.

Trent typed, *What is it?*

I made it.

Okay. What does it do?

Nothing.

Oh.

I have more. Bigger ones. Different things. More to show you.

Trent ran his finger over the surface of the glass. A blue glow surrounded the tip of his finger, pulsing through the glass of the object and coursing along the circuitry. Trent looked at the kid.

This does something.

Nope.

Can you try and make it work?

Squiggles shrugged. He glanced at the object. It sprang to life.

Blue fire ran under the glass, following the circuitry. It felt warm. Trent turned the yellow knob. The thing started humming. As he turned the knob, the pitch of the hum changed. He dialed it until there was a thrumming sound echoing through camp.

Can you hear that? He asked Squiggles.

Yes.

What does this do?

Nothing.

It does something.

Nope. But come see the rest.

The rest?

The boy smiled. Yes. I have something to show you.

Trent frowned. He looked at the weird machine in his hand. He had no idea what it did, or why he wanted it to do it. Trent thought about the last time he'd ventured into the restricted area.

I can't get caught where the soldiers told me not to go.

You won't get caught.

I will. They have cameras.

I turned them off.

What?

Yes. All of them. They won't work. No one will see. Come on, I have something to show you.

There's radiation.

No.

Yes there is. You can't see it, but it's there.

Safe. I go all the time.

Trent thought about that. It was true that the kid went in and out of the restricted area all the time. He showed no ill effects. Granted, super people could easily not be susceptible to radiation. But Trent was pretty sure that Squiggles would at least exhibit some signs of exposure. Maybe the professor was right about it being bullshit.

Trent looked at Squiggles. *This better be good.*

The super boy led Trent down the same path he had before. This time Trent went farther into the jungle. Squiggles took him off the path, slipping between two trees growing side by side.

They stepped down into a hidden valley. Fallen trees and palm bushes surrounded a bowl-shaped depression in the ground.

Squiggles slid down the bank to a stump near the middle of the sinkhole. He went around the side of the stump and disappeared. Trent followed. He found a hole in the roots of the fallen tree. He poked his head in and saw a light shining at the end of a short tunnel. Trent pushed his way through, crawling on hands and knees down under the stump.

He soon realized that he could stand. He walked toward the light until he found a wooden stair. Trent stepped into a circular room filled with shining dazzlement.

The walls were decked with sheets of polished metal that acted as mirrors—reflecting sunlight that came from an unseen source. A row of tubular missile casings filled with wires stood open along the far wall. Stacks of TVs and computer monitors were piled in various places throughout the wide, curved room.

Glass tubes, blocks of ceramics, computer banks, a jet-ski, an undersea mine, and rows of lights embedded in racks of metal caught Trent's eye. Wires, windows, tools, and copper tubing bedecked the walls. Through it all were thin bands of what looked like gold wire, laid in an intricate pattern that Trent recognized as more circuitry.

He opened his laptop. *What is this?*

What I wanted to show you.

Yeah, but what is it?

It's my fort.

And the stuff on the walls?

Just what I do. Decoration.

Trent smiled. He looked around the room. *It's more than that, Squiggles.*

More than this? Oh, yeah. This is just the top floor. Follow me. The boy opened what looked like a submarine hatch and disappeared into a dark hall.

Trent learned that there were several levels to the kid's fort. And five levels down, he figured out where they were.

He typed, *This is part of the military base.*

The what?

The place where the soldiers live.

The boy nodded. Yes. They lived here, too. Until three seasons ago. When they left, I took over. I gather decorations from the jungle.

Trent saw the same gold wire throughout the five levels of Squiggles' fort.

Tell me about this design.

It's the connection.

The what?

Connection. That's what it's called.

What does it do.

I don't know. Nothing?

Trent looked at the boy. He seriously doubted that was true. He followed the circuitry art back to the top level.

I like your fort.

Thank you. The boy beamed a smile.

Can we come back another time?

Yes.

Trent let the boy lead him back to camp.

Wednesday, June 23rd

Squiggles led me to his fort in the jungle. It's amazing!

He built it all from scraps, and there's circuitry and what I think might be working electronics. He did this without having any idea of his powers. I believe he can turn this fort on. I want to come back to it soon, and see what he can do.

This kid is a little genius.

Chapter Twenty-Five

Trent's balloon read, *Have you ever painted?*

Death Killer looked at the carving of the super woman he was showing Trent. *PAINTED?*

Put color on something to make a picture?

The villain frowned and shook his huge, horned head.

Trent took his notebook out and showed Death Killer some sketches he'd done while on the island.

Like this, but all colors, Trent ballooned.

Death Killer took the notebook from Trent and stepped away, tilting it into the light. He stared at the page, tracing lines with his claws. *GOOD!*

Thank you. It's what I really love to do. Trent rummaged in his bag until he found a pencil. He handed it to the super man. He blew up another balloon. It said, *Use this like your claw when you carve.* He pointed at the notebook.

The villain shoved the pencil straight through the notebook.

Trent took the notebook and pulled the pencil out. *More gentle. Light strokes, like this.* He demonstrated.

Death Killer took the stuff and scratched the pencil down the journal, tearing through several pages and breaking the pencil. He looked up at Trent with a frightened look on his masked face.

Trent smiled. *It's okay. I have more. You need a big brush.* Trent motioned for the notebook. He retrieved another pencil and sketched out what a paintbrush looks like, tapping the paper and holding up the balloon again. Then he ballooned the basics of paintbrush construction.

MAKE ONE! Death Killer's jagged bubble was thick

and bold, his pointy teeth shone. He took off into the sky, dropping the broken pencil at Trent's feet.

The student went off on his own artistic quest. He returned three hours later to find the villain planing logs with his claws. He showed Trent a stack of thin, square boards. Death Killer was creating his own sort of notebook. There was a stack of fairly well-constructed brushes of super villain size.

Trent showed him what he'd found. He took some berries, rocks, tree bark, roots, and flowers from his stuffed-full backpack. He wrote on balloons to ask the villain to gather other items like certain shellfish, and use his abilities to alter the materials.

When coconut bowls were filled with colors, Trent wrote, *These are paints.*

The villain smiled.

Trent walked along the row of paintings. He had some favorites. There were some of a certain super woman that were extraordinary. *I knew you'd shine with some color.*

Death Killer walked beside him. When they reached the end of the line, Trent told him about how well he was doing and a few things to think about. The villain nodded. He had a huge grin on his face that hadn't changed in hours.

He said, *Come inside.* His speech bubble was round and smooth.

The super villain lifted the boulder in front of his cave, and led Trent into his home.

Trent blew up a balloon and scribbled, *This is amazing!*

Death Killer smiled and motioned Trent further inside.

The walls, floor, and ceiling of the villain's spacious cave home were covered in a multitude of animal furs. The floor was plush and bouncy. Trent reached out and stroked thick black fur on the entryway. Death Killer showed him around.

The super man made tea and sat with the anthropologist

in his kitchen.

After some conversation where Trent noticed that the villain used only smooth, round speech bubbles—something Trent had never seen him do before—the student asked the question that had been on his mind most of all since he'd first encountered the super man.

Why do you live up here by yourself?

Death Killer sipped his tea, staring over it with knitted brows. Trent worried that maybe he'd overstepped his bounds.

I hate super people, the super man said. *Especially the do-goods, but the baddies, too.*

Why?

They're all stupid. They don't know why they do the things they do, but they do them anyway. Their minds are weak.

All of them?

Nearly all.

Trent looked at the imposing creature sitting across from him cross-legged on a giant warthog rug. *How long have you lived alone?*

Most of my life.

Did something happen?

Many things happened. Mostly ignorance.

Trent didn't press it.

The villain continued, *I loved a girl.*

Trent nodded.

A hero girl.

Trent nodded again, thinking of the paintings. He sat in silence as Death Killer's speech bubble dissipated. Finally he asked, *What happened?*

Stupidity happened. And death. I live here alone now.

Trent sipped his tea. He regretted asking.

Death Killer said, *Thank you for color.*

The student nodded. *You're welcome, Death Killer.*

You changed my life today. The bubble hung between them for nearly a minute.

Trent spent the rest of the evening with his new friend.

They talked about art concepts, girls, and blowing stuff up. Trent thanked the villain for saving him from the boar. Death Killer waved the thanks away with a warm smile.

The anthropology student left the mountain feeling that not only would he actually finish his study, but even make the professor proud.

Chapter Twenty-Six

Friday, June 25th

9:55 AM to Afternoon—picked up Death Killer for fishing trip. Explained about art of catching food with examples like fly-fishing and making lures from what you find in nature. He used a firebomb to explode the bay. Fish floated to the surface and he gave me thumbs up.

5:57 PM—Ate dinner with Death Killer. Blown up fish is pretty good.

7:05 PM—Made the mistake of telling DK about chocolate cake. He's out gathering supplies.

9:13 PM—Left Death Killer a note, he's still out collecting cake materials.

Saturday, June 26th

10:11 AM—DK was excited to have me taste the "cake" he'd "baked" the night before. Flamed or lasered iguana eggs, boar milk, crushed cocoa beans mixed with roots and some sort of vine juice, does not a chocolate cake make. I taught him about Bananas Foster.

2:04PM—Finally feeling better. Spent the past two hours puking.

5:49 PM—Ran across a pink bunny on trail. Death Killer picked it up and pet it. Then he skinned it with the flick of his wrist. Gave me thumbs up.

7:19 PM—Clam chowder. Should be sick again, but I'm fine.

9:38 PM—Did a shadow puppet show with pink bunnies for DK.

Tuesday, June 27th

8:20 AM—DK is up and out of his cave early. Will mix paint and wait for him.

11:09 AM—Went gathering ochre for yellow pigment with Death Killer. DK

113

walked straight path across island, blowing trees, rocks, even hills out of his way with heat vision and telekinesis. Fur, feathers, and foliage rained on us. Asked him to stop. He said, "What? I'm just making a trail."

Wednesday, June 28th

9:03 AM—Met with Squiggles in village and went to mud puddles. Spent the morning talking with him about the benefits of pumice and minerals. Took a mud bath with him.

11:17 AM—Poked stuff with sticks.

1:10 PM—With Squiggles at camp—playing video game on laptop that he made up. He controls it with his mind. It's about mud creatures and fighting ferns. I like it.

4:44 PM—Fern Fight!

6:23 PM—Finally stopped playing the game when I realized that Squiggles is asleep.

8:09 PM—Took the kid home.

Friday, June 30th

10:12 AM—Squiggles showed up at camp. Working with him on turning devices on and altering purposes—GPS locator makes decent music.

3:44 PM—Spent the whole day so far making sounds. Squiggles can make music with anything electronic. Have gathered stuff around camp for symphony.

6:53 PM—Kid performed for camp. Everyone loved it! Professor seemed impressed but distracted. Natalie tapped her foot.

8:08—Just finished having dinner with Squiggles. I really like that kid. Witnessed two separate fights between heroes and villains on the way back to camp.

Saturday, July 1st

12:20 PM—Going surfing with DK. He made us boards.

3:17 PM—DK and I witnessed fight between Whalemancer and a purple, starfish-looking villain. Starfish looked dead when we left. Didn't surf.

Sunday, July 2nd

8:34 AM—mud with Squiggles.

9:26 AM—poking.

1:11 PM—Fern Fight!!

2:12 PM—Just learned that Squiggles can control electronics from great distance. Had him prank call Martin on other side of island. Pretended to be hot super girl.

6:47 PM—HUGE BATTLE! There were seven or eight super people tearing the hell out of the jungle on my way home from Squiggles'. Had to take cover. What's going on? Fights are escalating in frequency.

Chapter Twenty-Seven

Professor Topper gathered the students in the morning to speak to them about the situation between the super people and some things that he and Natalie had learned.

He said, "Rivalries have escalated and tensions are extremely high. Both tribes have experienced missing individuals, and each tribe blames the other. But I believe there is something else going on. Just this morning I learned that there has never been a radioactive man born on the island. It appears that Colonel Shank is lying. Neither tribe is respo—"

A howling red, white, and blue man came crashing into camp from the sky. He hit the ground like a meteor, pushing out dirt-ripples and bouncing through Martin's tent. The hero rolled toward the anthropologists at the table. He came to a stop on his back—arms thrown wide open.

"Lightning Ray!" the professor shouted. He stumbled from the table.

They gathered around the fallen hero.

Lightning Ray was terribly injured. His left arm hung from his shoulder by a single glistening tendon. He had only one leg, and most of it was chewed off at the knee. His head looked dented and his mask bled thick black blood. He coughed—gurgling and hacking.

The professor blew up a balloon. *Lightning Ray, what happened?*

The hero raised his head and tried to talk.

A weak speech bubble oozed out of Lightning Ray's mouth. The bottom of the bubble filled with blood. It said, *They have Heat Vixen.*

Who does? Villains?

The speech bubble popped, splattering blood on the hero's chin. A weaker bubble read, *Unmasked.* It was hard to read—blood filled it rapidly.

Lightning Ray sputtered his last breath as his speech bubble burst, covering his face and upper body with blood, and splashing the professor, Trent, and Natalie.

"NO!" The professor lurched to his feet, dumping the mangled hero. He kicked through the gathered students, spitting and screaming. Tears streamed down his cheeks. "That bastard Shank is responsible for this!"

Trent rose, wiping blood from his cheek with his shirt. "The colonel did this?"

After a while the professor said, "I believe the military is responsible for the missing super people." He looked to Lightning Ray and wiped his tears. "I won't stand for this. I'm going to get that bastard off this island." He stalked across the camp toward the jungle.

"Professor!" shouted Natalie. She pushed up her glasses and ran off behind him.

The students stared after the professor and his assistant.

"Why would the military be involved with missing super people?" Martin asked.

Trent shook his head.

"What do we do?" Jen asked. She was crying.

Trent said, "I'm going after the professor. He's going to get himself in trouble."

"No. Don't go. Stay here." Jen took hold of Trent's belt loop. "There *is* going to be trouble. We should find a way to contact the University, or the boat…" She pulled at him.

"I'm going." He pried her finger off his pants.

"Me, too," Martin said. "We need to back-up the professor. I want to see what Shank has to say, anyway. Come on, let's go."

Trent looked at Jen. She stood crying, looking from the dead hero to each of her fellow students. He asked, "Coming?"

She shook her head, letting her hair cover her face.

"Okay." He said to Martin, "Let's go."

They jogged off into the jungle.

Jen stood and watched them go. She looked back at Lightning Ray.

She ran to catch up to Trent and Martin.

The professor stood in the path ahead of them, out in the tall grass. Colonel Shank, two cyber-troopers, and a squad of soldiers flanked him.

Professor Topper was screaming. "This is the most disgusting thing I've ever heard!"

The colonel said something the students couldn't hear.

"You can't be serious. Despicable."

More unintelligible words from the military man.

Trent stifled a sneeze.

"Well you can believe that I'm putting an end to this. I will be in contact with my superiors in the UN. I've already got communication lines opening. You'll be off this island in a matter of days, and you can be sure that I'll alert not only the governments of the world, but the media. That's right, you can expect to answer for your crimes on the evening news." The professor took Natalie by the arm and stormed away from the colonel.

Trent saw the anger in his teacher's face.

Professor Topper looked over his shoulder and yelled, "This isn't the last of me!" He and Natalie came straight toward the hidden students.

The colonel stood in the grass. Trent could see his smile. The military commander stared at the professor's back with icy eyes. He raised his hand and pointed.

Blue fire shot from the nearest cyber-trooper in two bursts.

Bolts of plasma blasted into the professor and Natalie, opening huge holes in their chests, which quickly spread—like a splash of acid eating the rest of their bodies. Trent saw the professor's wide-eyed surprise. Natalie yipped. And then they were gone.

Trent nearly screamed. He sat transfixed—gaping at the air where the professor had just been. Just beyond his focus, Colonel Shank and his machines stood admiring their work. Hard laughter rang across the clearing. Trent turned his head. He saw Martin in the shadows, his hand clamped over Jen's mouth. She kicked and struggled against the frat boy. He held her tight.

They kept quiet until the military men turned back toward their base. Then they ran like hell.

Chapter Twenty-Eight

Trent lagged to a stop behind Martin. Jen ran past and Trent grabbed her, pulling her down into a fern. She punched him and gouged at his face, screaming gibberish. He whisper-yelled for her to stop. Martin pulled Jen off and held her in a bear-hug while she kicked.

"Holy shit! Holy shit! Holy shit!" Martin chanted, getting a mouthful of Jen's hair.

"What the *fuck* just happened?" Trent asked, getting up and looking over his shoulder.

Jen stomped on Martin's foot. She jabbered when he let her go. "The professor's face. That—that—that—" She whirled and hugged the big frat boy, and burst into a fit of sobbing.

"I don't believe this," Trent said.

Martin met his eyes. "Believe it."

"We need help!" Jen shouted.

"Shh." They both hushed her.

Martin asked, "What the fuck do we *do*, man?"

Jen said, "We have to get off the island."

"The boat isn't coming until August," Trent said.

"Let's go back to camp," Martin said.

Jen pushed herself away from Martin. "You don't think they'll go there to kill us? They're going to kill us. They'll go there to kill us!"

"Calm down, Jen," Trent said. "She's right, though. They killed the professor and Natalie without a thought. They must know we'll wonder what happened to him. Shank might be on his way there right now to kill us."

Jen nodded, wiping tears from her face. "They killed them."

Martin asked, "Where are we going?"
Trent said, "Hero Village."

Before they arrived, the terrified students could tell something was going on in the village. They heard speech bubbles snapping like popcorn above the rush of their own heartbeats and breathing. When they came into view of the square, it was obvious something was wrong. The whole village seemed to be surrounding the well.

When they were closer, Trent noticed villains in the mix. Maybe all of Villain Village.

"What's going on?" Martin asked.

They slowed down and walked up to the well.

Speech bubbles, mostly jagged ones, were popping up all over. The super people were lined up like armies.

A big, red-suited villain with a blue mask and yellow cape pointed an orange-glowing finger and exclaimed with an angry bubble, *YOU did this. Give me back my Needleface!*

A hero replied, *No, you're the ones doing this.*

A small super woman who looked like a sexy skunk shouted, *Fuck you, hero douche!*

Trent saw one of the heroes who'd attacked Death Killer. His jagged bubble read, *It's* YOUR *fault!*

Madam Manifestor stood in the middle of the crowd. Trent couldn't read her bubble, but it gathered the super people's attention.

The red-suited villain responded to what she said. *Lies!*

The leader of the heroes floated down the line of super people until she was close to the villain. Trent could easily read her bubbles as she approached.

We have several pieces of evidence.

What evidence?

I'll speak to your leader about that.

You'll speak to all of us! You heroes are killing our people! The villain raised his fist. It glowed bright yellow.

121

Mustang Tornado jumped between Madam Manifestor and the villain. *You will show respect.*

Respect this! The villain answered. He threw a ball of yellow fire into Mustang Tornado's chest, knocking the hero backward into Madame Manifestor.

There was one second of electric stillness. Then chaos.

Fire, ice, plasma, dark matter, blades, hammers, pink flashes of light, and the pounding of super fists exploded in the village square.

A super woman in a green suit breathed some sort of gas into the crowd and heroes fell to their knees choking, flew off, or blinked out. A metallic heroine in a blue bikini bottom with a red and white half-shirt appeared behind her in a blur. She caught the green woman in a choke-hold, and another hero punched the villain in the gut.

A winged super man in a black and yellow suit shot out of the sky. His legs melded together at the knees and became a menacing stinger. A hero with rocky skin leapt from the crowd to meet the villain just as he was about to drive his venomous spear into a super woman punching at a yellow-green blob. The hero caught the wasp-man by the wings and pulled him backward into the ground.

Trent yelled, "Run!"

Martin was knocked to the ground by a tumbling hero. A tall villain in a purple suit stepped over Martin and kicked the hero. As he wound his foot up to do it again, he booted the frat boy on the backswing.

Jen screamed, "He's dead!" as Martin flopped on his face.

She tugged free of Trent's grip. Trent hadn't realized he was holding her arm. Martin sat up and rubbed his chin. Jen hugged him and pulled at him to stand.

"To the jungle!" Trent yelled, pointing at the dumbfounded duo.

They shook their stupors and fled.

Trent caught sight of Squiggles cowering under a burning hut wall that had fallen against the well. Flames burst around him as two fiery fighters battled beside him. A villain shining like the sun flew low over where Squiggles hid. Trent ran to save the boy. A jagged ray of lightning arced up and blasted the shiny super man.

Trent snatched up the boy as he rolled from his hiding place while shards of burning glass rained down around them and the wall he'd been under went up in one big whoosh.

Squiggles was hit on the hand by a burning piece of super villain and let out a jagged, ⸮ !

Trent held him tight and ran.

They fled fireballs, ice chunks, laser beams, and tumbling super people. Trent jumped over a smoldering hole by the big tree where they'd first stopped to observe the village. He let Squiggles down and they ran together toward the trees.

They met Jen and Martin on the trail in the jungle.

Jen sobbed, "What are we going to do now? We have nowhere to go."

A boulder whipped through the treetops just above the group, tearing trunks and branches apart. A fireball followed. Gouts of purple plasma struck the trees just in front of them, and a low rumbling sound fast approached.

"Run!" Trent yelled, tugging the boy along.

Trent realized they had to go to their camp. He led them there.

"What are we doing?" Jen shouted when they arrived. "You said not to come here."

"I need my laptop," Trent explained. "Gather stuff—food, equipment… just hurry." He ran to his tent.

On their way out of camp Jen said, "There's nowhere safe. What are we going to do?"

Trent told them, "I know a safe place to go."

There was a weird popping sound above them. A black hole opened in the sky and two super people fell out of it, dripping with an oily gunk that caught fire when one of the combatants used his power. The camp caught flame, the black oil burning hot blue. Once again, the group had to run.

Trent led them up a steep path to the summit of the mountain. He took them toward Death Killer's cave. He could see the villain painting.

Jen said, "What? You brought us to Death Killer? This is your safe place?"

"There's nowhere else to go. And this is the safest place on the island."

"I'd rather take my chances in the jungle."

Death Killer turned around, noticing them.

Trent waved to the villain.

The super man dropped his paintbrush. He flew to them, snarling.

Death Killer towered over Trent. *Why are you bringing these unmasked here? And a do-good! THEY ARE NOT WELCOME. LEAVE!*

Trent faced the villain and blew up three balloons. He had to ask Jen for a marker. *We have no place to go. War has erupted among the villages. And the military—Please, these are my friends. We're in danger.*

The super man glared at him and stalked back toward the painting he was working on. He spun around. *Keep that do-good away from my stuff.*

Martin stood staring at the villain.

Jen said, "I'm not staying here."

"He's not as bad as you think. And we'll be safe here."

Jen looked out off the side of the mountain. I don't think that's true. 'Looks like they're bringing the fight to the mountain." She pointed at a formation of flying figures.

Trent said, "They must be coming after Death Killer."

Martin said, "I think they're coming for us. Those are cyber-troopers."

The flying cyber soldiers banked and came rocketing fast.

Five giant robots flew straight for them. The students and

the little hero scattered, diving for cover and running behind rocks.

But the robot monsters ignored the anthropology students and their young super friend. They headed straight for Death Killer, who stood with his back to them, packing up his painting materials.

One of the military machines fired a continuous plasma beam into the back of the villain's head.

The blast shoved Death Killer straight into the cliffside, driving him into the rock. The villain struggled to escape the beam as the rest of the cyber-troopers surrounded him.

In an instant, the super villain stood behind the cyber soldier who'd been blasting him. Death Killer grabbed the huge machine by its leg and swung it like a plasma-gushing baseball bat. He connected with another of the advancing cyber-troopers, and sent them both careening over the side of the mountain and into the sea. The villain jumped straight into the air.

Two robot soldiers followed him, leaping into the sky.

Death Killer turned his laser eyes on one, slicing its weapon fists away and jabbing beams through its chest. It spun away in separate pieces, tumbling down the mountainside. He punched at the other when it closed a huge metal hand around him and squeezed. The villain and cyber-trooper plunged to the ground. Death Killer ripped its arm away and the thing teleported.

It reappeared directly behind the super villain and shot fire balls from its faceplate. Death Killer ducked under the volley of fire, and punched the cyber-trooper's head off. Its huge squarish body toppled to the ground.

One cyber-trooper remained. It flew at the villain in a twisting blur—lightning flying from its extended hands in huge jagged spears. It drove straight into Death Killer, doubling the villain over, and sending him smashing through a thick rock spire.

Death Killer rolled across the ground with boulders bouncing off of him. He tumbled within ten feet of the cowering students and lay still. Trent yelled. He jumped up to run to the fallen villain. Martin grabbed him by the shirt and pulled him to the ground.

"Don't be an idiot!" the frat boy yelled.

Trent watched the machine advance on his friend.

It raised its huge foot to stomp on the super villain.

Death Killer jumped up, grabbed the huge metal foot of the monster, and pulled it toward him. At the same time, he drove his super fist into the cyber-trooper's chest, shoving it straight through the metal soldier. When the villain withdrew his fist, it got caught up in the plating of the thing's chest. Death Killer shook his hand free, tearing off the chest plate, and throwing the cyber-trooper to the ground near the students.

Beneath the plating shone something terrible. Everyone could see it immediately.

It was a super man's torso. Blood and lubricant spurted from severed hoses and tubes. It poured out of the hole that the villain had made—coating the red suit. Blood splattered across a big white thumbs-up chest emblem. There were whirring and ticking sounds as gears spun and popped. Oil and bile sacs within the metal armor shivered and burst—their tubing filling with blood from the hemorrhaging super chest.

"What the *fuck*?!" yelled Martin.

Death Killer stood over the fallen trooper, staring at the flesh and blood super-chest under the woven metal and circuitry. Sparks snapped from the robotic armor. Its legs kicked and one of its metal arms jerked wildly. Then it hissed and fell still.

Jen stared at the dead cyber-trooper. She approached the fallen robot.

"Careful, Jen," Martin said.

"It's Fabulous Man," the girl said.

"What did you say?" asked Trent. He stumbled after Jen.

Jen knelt over the cyber-trooper. She pointed at the exposed super chest and stammered. She said, "Fabulous Man. It's Fab-Fabulous Man."

Death Killer stood over them, shaking gore off his hand.

Trent looked down at the super machine. "What is this?"

Jen bent beside the cyber-trooper's head. She pulled at the faceplate, digging her nails into the metal seams, beating at the glass and crying. "Get it off! Get it off!" she shrieked.

Death Killer reached down and pulled off the faceplate.

Fabulous Man was under there, his sightless eyes open. One socket had a metal cube with blinking blue buttons where his eyeball should have been and frayed wires sticking out of it. The other was a white, dead eye. His shaved head was pale, and looked partly pickled. A long scar made a "T" across his brow and up over his skull. Wires protruded from puss and blood holes at the super man's temples. Their torn ends sparked. Jen wept, hugging the dead hero's head to her chest.

Martin said, "Cyber-troopers are super people."

Jen screamed. She fell to sobbing.

Trent held her and cried, too. Finally, he said, "Come on. Let's move."

Martin helped them up.

Death Killer followed them toward a pile of boulders away from what was left of Fabulous Man.

They stumbled past another dead cyber soldier, the one with the missing head. Thick blood seeped from its neck.

Trent looked up at Death Killer. He fished a balloon out of his pocket and found the inside of a broken marker. He wrote, *They were coming for you.*

I know. They always do, the villain answered.

Death Killer wandered toward his cave.

Chapter Twenty-Nine

Fires burned below the mountain. Hero Village was marked by a plume of thick black smoke and flashes of pink, red, and yellow light. Explosions sounded across the southern half of the island—little pockets of fighting left mushrooms of flame and fumes dotting the jungle. The sky was busy with flying super people, laser beams, ice bolts, and various other projectiles.

Jen's glossy eyes looked to Trent with glossy eyes. She said, "They're going to destroy everything. They'll kill each other. If they only knew that it's the military behind it. If they knew the truth…"

Trent said, "We need to make a plan." He turned and looked for Death Killer. He found the villain stalking around near the front of his cave. The super man pulled a ruined sculpture from the ground and watched it dangle in his claw.

"We could find some super hottie to fly us the fuck outta here," Martin said.

Jen said, "The professor was killed. We can't let them get away with this. They're killing super people. Fabulous Man! And all of them. We have to protect these people. Think of how many cyber-troopers there are. You told us, Martin. Inside each one…" Her eyes welled-up.

Squiggles pointed at Trent's pack. **?**

Trent nodded. He pulled the laptop out.

Martin said, "We could build a boat."

Jen said, "We have cameras. We need to document what's happening here. We need to get the truth out about cyber-troopers. We need to stop this. We need to make the military pay for what they're doing."

Martin said, "Are you fucking kidding me? You saw those things in action. I know all about those monster machines. I'm not going up against the fucking military. We have to find a way off this goddamned island!"

Trent's laptop warmed up. Squiggles asked, *Are we going to die?*

He looked at the kid—his little shiny bald head, and big innocent eyes.

"No," he said, shaking his head and typing the word. "No, we're not leaving. We have to help these people."

Chapter Thirty

Martin videotaped Jen. She said, "I'm Jennifer Giesch. I'm an anthropology student on the Island of the Super People. We are in the middle of a violent battle between the heroes and villains of the island. The fight started over a terrible truth we've only just uncovered." She motioned for Martin to film the cyber-trooper that had been Fabulous Man.

He did, and went back to Jen. "It is the military that's the cause of this situation. Cyber-troopers are super people! The military has been abducting people from this island and turning them into their cybernetic soldiers. They are killing these innocent super people to make them into weapons. That was my friend." She pointed at the dead hero, wrapped in his metal shell. "Think of how many of these machines are out there. Each one is a dead islander." Martin panned-out.

Jen said, "We are going to try and stop the war between the heroes and villains. We're going to put an end to this disgusting scheme of the military's. Look at what they've done." She waved toward the battles raging below them.

Martin filmed the area—the cyber-strewn battleground on top of the mountain, and the action happening below them. He captured an aerial fight between two freeze-powered super people. He stopped filming as one plummeted into the jungle.

Trent said, "Good. Okay. Now we've got to convince the super people to stop fighting."

"Good luck with that. Have you looked around?" Martin pointed toward the smoke and flashes coming from Hero Village.

"We have to try," Jen said.

"Oh, we'll do more than try." Trent said. He went to talk to Death Killer.

The villain said, *Don't care.*

Death Killer let Trent know in no uncertain terms that he was not interested in helping them stop the fighting. He worried about his mangled art and complained about Squiggles being there. When Trent pushed the issue, the villain flashed his eyes and snarled.

Trent went back to the students. He said, "We're on our own." He pointed at Fabulous Man. "We'll take him down there and show them what's going on."

"The big guy's not gonna help us?" Martin asked.

Trent shook his head.

Jen asked, "Will they listen to us?"

"They'll have to."

Martin said, "You want us to carry that thing down the mountain?"

"Don't be a pussy," Jen said. She went to the fallen hero-soldier and hefted one of his shoulders.

Trent took the other side of the cyber-hero's upper body. They started to drag it toward the path down.

"Ah, fuck. You can't do it by yourselves." Martin grabbed hold of the gray metal monster boots and lifted.

Squiggles followed.

Getting the body down the mountain was no easy task. They struggled with it as fighting went on nearby—bursts of fire, ice, or some other deadly material fell around them as they dragged, pulled, and rolled the large metal body toward the heat of the battle.

The students came to a clearing and found a small skirmish.

Super people faced-off in tight lines. Fists and feet flew. Blood and teeth mixed with freeze rays, plasma droplets, and burning bees of super-fire. Heroes flew and were thrown. Villains fell under mighty stone fists and stood inside violet flames throwing black stars of gelatinous space-time.

Trent led the students straight to the center of the fighting. They staggered over a writhing snake-person squeezing the air from a spiny, red, white, and blue woman. Super people noticed the intrusion onto their battlefield, and the fighting lagged.

The students let momentum drive them as far into the fighting as possible, and dropped the body to the ground between the two sides. The cyber-trooper's arms fell to its sides as it thumped into the dusty field, exposing the white thumbs-up.

It took only a moment for the fighting to die completely as both sides looked down at the thing between them—the mix of super person and unmasked machine. A wave of silence rippled through the battle. A circle formed around Fabulous Man.

Speech bubbles popped off—*What is the meaning of this?*

Fabulous Man!

Fabulous?

The thumbs up!

Those unmasked machines.

A tall villain woman in a black suit with a red cape and mask raised her arms and screeched like a falcon. The bubbles stopped.

Trent saw that Madame Manifestor was there. She pushed through the crowd to the body.

Jen had a balloon blown up. She shoved some at Martin. "Blow these up."

She wrote on the balloon and held it up, turning slowly so everyone could read it. It read, *You need to stop fighting—* She held her hand out to Martin. He finally understood and handed her another balloon. He blew the rest up.

Trent gathered blown-up balloons to hand to Jen.

Jen wrote, *—each other! You are not enemies!*

Trent handed her a balloon.

Your REAL enemies are the—

—unmasked who did this!

They make heroes AND villains—

—into these machines.

We have to stop them.

132

Together we can.

The super people looked at Jen. They glanced around at each other. Many could not keep their eyes from Fabulous Man.

Squiggles hid behind Trent.

Madam Manifestor finally spoke. Her bubble was big and fat. It hung for a long time.

You're only an unmasked. How can we believe you? And how could such little things capture one of us? No, I believe it is the villains who have done this.

Jen scribbled on the next balloon. *See for yourselves. Go to their base!*

A deep boom sounded in the distance. Huge super bodies tensed and powers flared.

Do not assume to tell me what to do, said Madame Manifestor.

Please! Jen answered.

The super people stood ready to continue their battle.

Squiggles crouched behind Trent. Madame Manifestor looked imposing and terrible. Her face was pocked with rage. Villains were poised to pounce on her. Eyes flashed, light flared. Then the little hero stood straight up, as if buoyed by an unseen hand.

Jen's next balloon read, *Look at Fabulous Man! Look at him! The villains did not do that.*

Of course they did, answered the super heroine.

Jagged speech bubbles erupted from both sides.

Jen let the balloon in her hand fall. It gently bounced off the thumbs-up on Fabulous Man's exposed chest.

Martin said, "Yup."

Squiggles stepped beside Trent. A wave of super people rose before them, building itself back into a crashing force. Jagged speech bubbles filled the air. The boy looked to Trent.

Trent stared at the super people working themselves up to battle again. He reached out to Jen. Squiggles snatched the laptop from his hand and flipped it open. The super boy climbed onto the cyber-trooper and raised the computer over his head.

133

The laptop's screen was filled with a Squiggle-style electro-speech bubble. In huge bold print was the word, *STOP!*

Bubbles dissipated.

The words on the laptop changed. *These unmasked speak the truth! Listen to them! It is the military unmasked who steal our people. They use our powers as weapons and lock our bodies inside these machines. We must stop them!*

Madam Manifestor said, *And why should we listen to you, Captain Fuckup? You have no powers. You are barely more a person than the unmasked.*

Bubbles of agreement inflated around them.

Squiggles closed the laptop and handed it down to Trent. The super boy dropped to his knees on the cyber-soldier and began pulling parts off of the metal body.

In a blur, he assembled bits and pieces of the cyber-trooper into a knobby sphere the size of a softball. Lights blinked across its surface, sections of it separated, slid, and reconnected. It hummed and beeped. Squiggles opened his hand and let the sphere go. It took off flying through the gathered crowd, shooting little sparks at the ones who got too close to it.

The metal ball hovered above the crowd. A triangle-shaped opening appeared in its side, with whirling blue lights around it. A holographic speech bubble shot from the opening, unfurling with a flash of rainbow light. It was white, with black lettering, just like a real one.

It read, *Listen to these unmasked. What they say is true. And stop calling me Captain Fuckup. My name is Squiggles.*

The sphere returned to Squiggles, who reached up and caught it in both hands.

He smiled.

Other super people smiled. There were confused and excited looks exchanged.

Jen said, "Go, Squiggles!"

"Cool," Martin said.

New bubbles popped up among the super people. They couldn't believe the boy had done what he'd done. They took long looks at the dead cyber-trooper. They came to Squiggles, and touched him, speaking to him for the first time, ever. Villagers from both sides agreed to listen to what the little hero had to say.

With his spherical speech bubble machine, Squiggles went to work convincing each side to rally their people to attack the military base.

Chapter Thirty-One

Jen left with the super villains to Villain Village to inform the rest of them about the truth of the situation. They took the body of Fabulous Man with them. Martin went with the heroes—Madam Manifestor's word would convince them.

Trent and Squiggles climbed back up the mountain.

Death Killer was arranging huge paint-boards near his cave. There were buckets of paint out, and the bone sculpture that appeared to be repaired.

Squiggles sat down on the far side of the clearing with the laptop.

Trent approached the villain with a balloon held up. *We need your help.* He blew up another balloon as the villain shook his head no.

Trent said, *Fighting the military.*

NO.

Please. You are strong. We need you. Your people need you.

Not interested. Have idea for art project.

Trent shook his head. He blew up another balloon. *You can save lives.*

Not worth it. Let them die.

You won't help your people be free?

Not my people.

But they're being killed. Turned into weapons and slaves.

DON'T CARE.

I care. Help for me?

No. Not for you. Have an idea for painting.

I thought we were friends.

Death Killer frowned at Trent and popped his balloon.

"Hey!"

Squiggles' sphere floated between the villain and the student. A holographic bubble flashed out. *Death Killer, please help us.*

Lasers shot from Death Killer's eyes. The sphere burst into sparks and fell to the ground, cleaved in half.

Squiggles popped his head up from behind a boulder and ducked down quickly.

Trent blew up another balloon. *They need your help!*

The villain popped the balloon.

As my friend!

Death Killer popped it and took a step closer to the student. His eyes flashed.

Trent inflated a balloon through tears. He scribbled on it while Death Killer clenched his clawed fists and snorted.

Trent held up the balloon.

Death Killer popped it without reading it.

Trent threw the deflated balloon. "Fine then! I'll do it on my own!" He kicked the bone statue, knocking off a femur.

He stormed away to gather Squiggles, tears stinging his eyes.

The villain stared after him and then began gathering bones.

Trent ran down the mountain trail. He hoped Jen, Martin, and their groups of super people would be more successful in obtaining help. He tried not to think about Death Killer and hoped he'd never see him again.

Chapter Thirty-Two

The staging area was a gully between two long ridges. A gentle slope led to the ridge that faced the military base. A steeper slope faced it. Bunkers and a command post stood near the top of the ridge.

Heroes and villains formed a mass of color and ability in the valley. They swarmed the staging area, flitting between trees, floating above the grass, and mingling warily with each other. The two sides met to fight as one—against a real enemy.

Tension flexed a thick muscle in the bodies and minds of the converging army. Rivals nodded cautiously across the field at each other. There was jostling and jeering, but nothing serious.

Each side was beginning to really let go of the idea that the other was responsible for the disappearances of their friends and family. Their anger was turning. Shock and amazement that the unmasked could accomplish such feats rippled through the ranks. Wrath pushed its way to the forefront.

Trent and Squiggles arrived as Martin and Jen were filming an interview with the leaders of the villages. They were on the slope just below the command post. The flame-head guy—Big Burner—stood beside Madam Manifestor.

Jen spoke to the camera, hoping beyond hope that the message she recorded would make its way off the island and to the people of the world.

"People of the world, the military has been exploiting and systematically destroying the men and women from the Island of the Super People for years now. It's not only a despicable practice, slaughtering the islanders to make them into cyber-slaves, but it's caused a war between the villages. Many lives have been lost already, and more stand to be lost in the coming battle to liberate the island from the invading army.

"We want to learn the viewpoints of the leaders of the villages about what's been happening and what's about to happen. We're going to battle, and we'd like the world to know why from the people whose lives are at stake."

Martin filmed the gathering army while Jen inflated a balloon and then went back to the interview.

Jen held up a balloon to Madam Manifestor. *Madame, in your eyes, what has been happening here?*

Madam Manifestor answered in a huge, jagged bubble. *War! The unmasked are killing our people. We will not stand for it.*

Big Burner joined her in condemning the military. They spoke of the professor being murdered by Colonel Shank, and of the discovery of cyber-troopers being mutilated super people. Big Burner and Madame Manifestor swore to free their island, no matter what it took. The interview was quick and concise—spelling out what was going on from the view of the islanders. Jen summarized the situation, explaining that they would tape as much of the coming battle as they could.

Trent sent Squiggles with his laptop to inform the troops about all he knew about what to expect from the cyber-troopers.

When the interview ended, Martin noticed Trent standing there, gawking at the scene. "Shit yeah, right? Can you believe we got all these fuckers together?"

Jen said, "Trent! We did it! Check it out."

He was indeed checking it out. Trent saw every hero and villain he'd seen since he'd arrived on the island—and hundreds more. There were super people as far as he could see. They stood shoulder to shoulder along the hillside and floated beside each other for nearly a thousand yards in either direction. Rock fists, swamp faces, claw hands, spiked bodies, capes, masks, glowing balls of super energy, giants, bug-swarms, metal heads, drill feet, rubber extremities, shimmering invisibles, plasma orbs, and so many other assorted super sights stood together that Trent felt like he was inside a video game.

Jen asked, "How did it go with Death Killer?"

Trent shook his head. "He was a total dick. He even destroyed that translator Squiggles built. I had to give the kid my laptop to talk to these people."

"Great," Martin said. "We could have really used the big guy."

"We'll do fine without him," Jen said. "Let's go over some planning with the leaders, okay Trent?"

He nodded and followed her to the command post. He was introduced to the leader of the villains.

Big Burner said, *Thank you for your discovery.*

He nodded and inflated a balloon. *I'm happy both peoples listened.*

Yes. It is still sinking in—what the unmasked are doing. This has been happening for several cycles now. There has been bad blood between our villages—beyond our natural divergences.

Madame Manifestor asked, *Do you know the strengths of these machines?*

They are super people AND machines. I fear they are very powerful.

We will surprise them. Destroy their base. Big Burner smacked his fiery fist into his flaming palm.

Trent told them, *Five fought against Death Killer. He defeated them, but not easily.*

Death Killer! Big Burner's speech bubble was jagged. *He is nothing.*

Madame Manifestor said, *He is the strongest of all of us. But if he can take five, our army can take five hundred.*

Trent blew up two balloons. *It may need to. We have no idea how many of them are on the island. There are many in the world.*

Madam Manifestor threw her hands in the air. *Our people*

leaving this island!

Parts of them. Big Burner's head flared big and bright. *Come. Let us crush these intruders!*

The villain marched off along the side of the ridge. Jagged bubbles shot around his head. The super people pumped their fists and flared their powers. Bubbles erupted through the ranks—most were strong and jagged.

Squiggles wove through the super people, laptop held high. Many of the heroes and villains reached out to touch the boy as he passed. There was a palpable energy coming from the crowd beyond their powers. There was fear, and anger, and hate.

"This is so fucked," Trent said.

The base looked quiet. Trent scanned the squat rectangular buildings and their surrounding grounds with his binoculars. Cyber-troopers and soldiers milled about or marched in lines. Some cyber-troopers were digging a trench near one of the buildings.

Trent saw Colonel Shank. He stood in the shade of a palm tree with two cyber-troopers and a few soldiers. He was smoking his cigar and throwing his head back to laugh.

"What is the plan, Martin?"

"We're gonna send two waves of fliers at it first. Bombers—like fire people, ice, magma, rocks, plasma, lightning... The second wave will be more of the same and some fliers with payload—metal and rock people, an acid guy, smaller tough super folk that can hit the ground hard and get up kicking ass. Once they're down, the flanks move in—ground forces, air, and tunnelers. Then we tear that place apart."

"They know they've gotta gang up on those cyber things, right?"

"They know."

Trent tapped Squiggles on the shoulder and typed, *Do*

your people understand how powerful the machines are?
I told them what I saw.
Good. Trent nodded.

"Are they ready?"

Martin looked at the line of super people. The sun shone in patches through the trees at their backs. Fearsome, beautiful women with murder in their eyes and breasts of all shapes and hue. He saw flame-head facing him.

Groups of fliers and their bombs for the second wave of the attack waited on the ridge behind outcroppings like their makeshift command post. The first lines of tunnelers and super-fast runners were up top, too.

Martin told Trent, "They're ready."

Jen said, "Let's fuck these assholes up."

Trent stepped out from the rocks and looked down at the gathered super people. He thought, *I hope this works.*

He waved his arm toward the base.

Seventy-eight super people rose from the ranks and flew toward the base—dividing into groups and banking off to gather speed and attack from all angles.

Trent and Jen watched the base through binoculars. Martin used the camera's viewscreen.

Colonel Shank smiled at the sky. His cigar clamped between his teeth.

"What's he up to?" Trent asked.

"Who?" Martin wondered. He was watching a sexy black-suited chick flying around in purple fire. She had the sweetest, tightest ass of any super woman he'd seen.

"The colonel."

Jen and Trent trained their binoculars on the base leader—Martin zoomed the camera. Colonel Shank stood in the open, watching the super people streaming from the sky at full speed, straight for him. He kept smiling. The cyber-troopers by his side remained at ease.

Super people rushed toward the base—some of them breaking the sound barrier. As sonic booms reverberated and a rain of super anger opened up above the military man and his base, Colonel Shank spoke casually into a walkie-talkie.

"Fuck!" Trent yelled. "Call them off. Call them off!"

Martin said, "What?"

Streaking from the sky, and just opening fire, the super people met the cause of the colonel's casual attitude. In a blink, a crackling-blue energy field surrounded the base with a whirling dome of electrified plasma.

The fliers dropped like flies when they hit the force field.

Heroes and villains rammed the sparking blue shield like bugs on a windshield. They splatted and bounced. They fell along the burning dome, thumping to the ground outside its perimeter.

"Oh my God!" Jen yelled.

None of the fallen super people were moving.

The leader of the tunnelers let fly a jagged bubble and all of the earth-movers went underground—burrowing for base. Trent hoped they'd get under that shield and show those inside how stupid a dome is against tunnelers and teleporters.

But nothing happened. They never popped up inside.

The teleporters blinked out and snapped right back. Most were dazed, six were unconscious. None appeared inside the crackling blue dome.

"Shit," Trent said. He typed, *Get Big Burner up here!*

Squiggles ran down the ridge with the laptop.

He returned quickly, followed by the rest of the troops. They rushed to the top of the ridge, just in time to witness the aftermath of the failed attack.

Trent focused on the colonel through the blue fire of the shield. He was laughing.

Movement along the edges of the swirling blue shield caught his attention.

Huge machines that looked like scorpions with tank-tread legs and no heads came from five wide holes in the ground around the base. Long, jointed arms stuck off the sides of their flat backs. They were like robot trucks tricked-out to look like scary bugs. With claw arms.

The scorpion things drove out of the force field—passing through it like it was a thick soap bubble. They began gathering the super people lying around the dome. The metal arms scooped them up and dumped them on their truckbed backs. The scorpions wheeled back through the shield.

Trent saw the bugbots pouring toward the center of the base from all sides. They took their cargo back down the holes.

"This is fucked," he said.

Jen said, "We have to disable that shield."

Chapter Thirty-Three

The super people stood staring down at the base. The scorpion vehicles disappeared down their holes.

Big Burner turned to Trent. *This is a bad thing.* He and Madam Manifestor walked along the ridge-top, gathering a crowd as they walked.

"He's right," Martin said. "A fucking *shield*?"

Jen asked, "What can we do about it?" She watched the base.

"I'm thinking," Trent told her. He worried that cyber-troopers would come pouring through the shield at any minute.

"Do you think the bald kid could drop the shield?"

Trent looked at Martin. "He might be able to."

He typed, *Do you think you can disable the shield?*

I don't know. What is a shield?

I need your help, come with me.

Trent closed the laptop.

"What are you going to do?" Jen asked.

"We're going down there to take out that force field. When it goes down, hit 'em with everything we've got left."

"You shouldn't go anywhere near that thing!"

Trent didn't answer. He ran down the ridge, dodging rocks and trees. Squiggles came behind him.

The dome crackled and hummed up close.

Squiggles walked straight for the swirling blue wall of

energy. Trent snatched him by the cape.

?

Trent typed, *That shield could kill you. Don't touch it. Look at those trees.* He pointed to smoldering branches on trees at the perimeter of the shield.

The boy looked at the trees, and then the dome.

Can you do anything to make the shield go away?

Squiggles stood and stared at the wall of energy. He put his hands to his little bald head and squeezed his eyes tight.

No. I'm sorry. He gasped for air.

Try accessing the computer inside that controls it. He said out loud, "We've *got* to drop that shield."

I can't do it, Squiggles said.

How about anything outside that might control it? Can you find any fuse boxes, or electrical relays or anything?

The boy closed his eyes. After a while he said, *Nothing.*

Okay. Trent stared up at the curving force field. He looked through the swirling energy at the base. He knew they'd taken all the super people inside for a reason. He moved to get a different angle on the nearest building.

Trent stumbled over a root and fell toward the sizzling field of energy. He threw back his hand for balance, and Squiggles caught it. The boy didn't grab hold soon enough stop Trent's fall. But when Trent opened his eyes, he found that he was hanging halfway through the force field.

Squiggles stood outside of the blue wall, holding Trent's left hand in both of his, feet planted wide. Trent's upper body pushed through the shield, the laptop dangling near the ground inside the perimeter. He shouted, arching his back.

The boy pulled, and they tumbled back into the jungle.

Trent lay there and caught his breath. He pulled the laptop to his chest and typed, *I was partway through the shield.*

Yes.

How?

I don't know.

Circuitry.

What?

Never mind.

Trent sat up. He looked at the humming blue wall. His heart slowed. His hands shook less.

He typed, *I think you can go through the shield. And it seems that if you touch me, I can, too.* He sat and stared at the crackling blue energy field. *I think we can get through there and shut the shield down. But I want to try something. I'll hold you, and you put your hand on the shield. See if you can push it through. But be careful. I'll pull you off if it zaps you.*

Okay.

The stood up and faced the dome.

Squiggles put his hand over the crackling blue energy, and braced himself. He squeezed Trent's fingers in his, and reached out to touch the shield. Nothing happened. The super boy pushed his hand straight through. He smiled and wiggled his fingers on the other side of the blue energy.

Trent let go of the boy, and the little hero put his whole arm in.

No problem.

Trent typed. *Yeah, no problem.* He shook his head and wiped some sweat away. *Okay. We can do this. We have to. It's up to us. Let's try it again. You hold my hand. We walk through.* He didn't type the thought, *And hopefully we won't die.*

Okay.

Okay. But first we need to decide where to go once we're in there. Trent looked around the base. Men ran between buildings, and a couple of those scorpion vehicles drove in and out of holes in the ground.

Trent typed, *We need to find some place to deactivate the shield. Maybe we just need to get you closer to its source. I don't know. We'll find a way. I have a feeling most of this base is underground, most military bases are. And there's not much above ground, so we'll look for ways down that don't involve going down a scorpion hole. You control any electronics that might harm us, or see us, or sound alarms.*

Squiggles nodded, watching the movements of men and machines in the compound beyond the blue fuzz of the shield. There was not much activity. Not a single cyber-trooper patrolled or stood guard.

The two devised a general plan that involved running to the closest building. Trent hoped they'd make it out once they were in.

Chapter Thirty-Four

Trent stared at the shield. He smiled warily at his small friend and took his hand. "We're probably going to die." He closed his eyes.

They stepped into the blue toward a clump of shimmery palm trees.

Trent opened his eyes on the other side. He squeezed the boy's hand and then let go to type, *We made it!*

Squiggles smiled.

Soldiers stood outside the building. Trent pointed at them. Squiggles nodded. An alarm began to sound in the helicopter that sat nearby. The soldiers looked to each other and ran across the field to the chopper. Squiggles grabbed Trent by the hand again and pulled him toward the windowless building in front of them.

Leaning against the building, Trent typed, *Now we find a way inside.*

He scooted along the wall until he came to the corner. Trent peered around and found no one in sight. He led Squiggles around the building and up a short flight of concrete stairs to a door. Too late, he saw the security camera above it. He ducked, as if the camera would shoot him.

Squiggles shook his shoulder. He pointed at the camera, smiling. **?**

Trent made knife-across-the-throat motions with a questioning shrug.

The kid nodded.

Trent tried the door. It was locked. "Shit!"

Squiggles smiled and the electronic lock hummed and clicked open.

Trent nodded.

They ducked into a long, empty hall with doors running along either side. Trent tried the first door on his left. It opened.

It was an office.

A small metal desk was topped with a widescreen computer monitor and an ashtray stuffed with cigarette butts.

Trent opened his laptop. *See if you can turn off the shield here.*

The computer monitor on the desk came on. Squiggles' avatar appeared on the screen. An electro-speech bubble popped out of its little digital mouth. *Let's find out how!*

Digital Squiggles ran his finger across the desktop monitor, drawing a white line along the screen. He grabbed the line with both hands and pulled it apart. Light shone from the crevice the little avatar hero created. He reached into it and pulled out a file folder.

The file opened to fill the screen.

Schematics of the shield appeared. Trent tried to make sense of them. He saw that it reached deep underground and formed a capsule around the whole base. The underground was a vast network—something like ten or fifteen levels deep. It looked like there were two big things somewhere that were connected to something that had something to do with the shield.

Trent typed on the laptop. *Can you understand this stuff?*

Squiggles nodded, both in the office standing beside Trent, and on-screen. The avatar Squiggles closed the file and ran toward the edge of the computer screen. He leapt off-screen and appeared on the laptop. He placed the file there.

The real Squiggles seemed to almost glow. His bald head gained a green tint, and his eyes flared extra white. He put a hand to his head.

Are you okay?

Yes. Dizzy. There is a great deal of information here.

Onscreen, the little guy jumped back into the military computer and gathered more files. He was holding them in his digital hands and dropping them at his pixel feet. Then he got the bright idea to just vacuum the files out in a steady stream, straight onto the laptop.

Trent typed, *What are you doing?*

Transferring files. There's a map there of the entire underground facility. There are files on no less than seventeen sub-sections of three separate programs involving the harvesting of super people parts. And many more files. And access to a worldwide network. So much information...

I've found how to disable the shield, but I must be within closer proximity. There are security measures against remote access that I cannot penetrate from here—shielding against just this sort of threat. I have scrambled all surveillance, and opened all the locks. I have access to the security system, as well as every other system on base. All personnel files are open. I know the enemy. I can get us there. We have to leave this building right now, through the opposite door from where we came in. Keep the laptop open. Let's go.

The boy turned and ran through the door.

Trent said, "Squiggles?" and followed.

They ran across the field and into a small metal shack. A scorpion vehicle rounded the corner of one of the cinderblock buildings while they were in the open. It raised a menacing claw and sped toward them. Trent could see a gun barrel spinning inside the metallic talons. The scorpion bore down on them, veering off at the last moment, braking quickly, and powering down. Squiggles nodded, pulling Trent along. He yanked the door open and ducked inside. Trent followed, slamming the door closed. The floor dropped.

Trent yelled.

Be quiet now. We're dropping seven levels—about a quarter-mile below the surface.

A map appeared on the laptop—a blueprint-type schematic complete with a flashing green dot representing them and a big red target light glowing below them through a few sideways tunnel-things.

Squiggles, you seem very suddenly different.

I feel suddenly different.

Just as Trent's stomach caught up with him, and he became accustomed to the rate of their fall, the platform stopped moving, and a door opened in front of them. Squiggles grabbed Trent's hand and pulled him down the hallway and into an alcove. He pointed.

Two guards flanked a wide door down the hall.

The super boy said, *I'll make them leave.*

Each of the guards put a hand to their ear, receiving orders through their earbuds, and looked at each other. They ran down the hall the opposite direction.

They won't be gone long. Let's go.

Squiggles led Trent toward the door. It opened and they ran through.

A long, white, sterile hall stretched before them.

They ran along it.

Squiggles suddenly stopped. Trent crashed into him and they tumbled. The laptop went skittering down the hall.

After assuring that the boy was okay, Trent retrieved the laptop. It seemed to be working. He turned to find Squiggles disappearing through a doorway.

Trent caught up to him inside a wide, well-lit room. They stood in a gritty shop of horrors filled with the stench of death and rot.

The little hero was welded to the spot, shaking. A jagged bubble popped beside his head.

Super people bodies hung from hooks on either side of the walkway, slowly twisting and swaying. Headless torsos with roughly hacked-off limbs and flayed-open skin littered the room. Some bodies had a whole arm or leg, and a few had heads, or pieces of them.

Skinned, bloody bits of muscle and sagging flesh hung from grisly hooks. Chipped bones, frayed tendons, and shrunken worms of blood vessels and gristle poked out of raggedy stumps. Strings of shredded entrails swayed and stuck together above Trent's head. Blood pooled in square basins below the tattered bodies. The floor was spattered with blood and bits of hair and meat.

Directly in front of Trent stood a table full of hacked-off

capes and cowls of all colors and size. Some were old and stiff-looking, others were fresh and gory—draped over the gristled piles stacked high on the table. Blood dripped off its edges.

Squiggles had recovered enough to stagger down the aisle, staring at the mutilated bodies twisting on their hooks.

The boy slipped in a yellow puddle under the severed head of a super woman suspended from a braided strand of wires that ended inside her skull, and fell into a gurney with a sheet draped over the body on top of it.

The sheet fell away, revealing a dissected super villain— his black suit torn open down its middle and only a shallow pool of blood with spine islands inside the gaping hole. The body smelled bad. Squiggles staggered backward into some opaque plastic hanging like a shower curtain around a hospital bed. The super boy was covered in yellow gunk, and splashed it everywhere. His crazy speech bubbles popped around him.

As the sheeting fell away, Trent saw a familiar super woman in the bed.

Heat Vixen lay on a bloody sheet, her body torn in half— guts falling out below her tattered ribcage. A clear plastic bag was stapled to her body. It contained her organs. It was filled with steam, blood, and shifting guts as her backbone snaked around inside, twitching like the severed tail of a lizard. Her left eye was missing. Its socket was pooled with pus and blood. Wires protruded from a shaved patch on that side of her scalp. They led to a bank of beeping machines beside the bed.

She was alive. And she was awake.

A bloody speech bubble slid from Heat Vixen's bruised-black lips. *They stole my powers.* She raised her left arm to reveal a bandaged stump where her hand had been. Blood soaked the bandage.

Squiggles and Trent stumbled to her side, the boy slipping and spreading yellow goo over the floor.

Trent searched for a balloon and marker.

Heat Vixen said, *Kill me.*

The student met her eye. He shook his head.

Yes. The bubble was half-filled with blood. When it popped, it sprayed them all.

Trent put his hand on the super woman's shoulder. He looked into her steely eye and took her remaining hand in his.

Please. The bloody bubble splashed them when it burst. Stuff sloshed out of Heat Vixen's eye socket as she tried to raise her head.

Trent looked to the boy. Terrible resolve passed between them.

Squiggles nodded. Tears leaked down his cheeks. He wiped them and the blood from his face. He waved his hand at the machine hooked to the heroine's face.

Heat Vixen's eye went wide. She tried to speak as her torso convulsed and her guts slid further onto the bed, puffing up the plastic bag. Her spine beat her organs to pulp in its nerve-pulling death throes. She gasped. Blood poured from her eye-socket and dribbled across her cheek into her ear.

The boy cried. He threw himself on the heroine's body.

Trent stared at the super woman, wiping blood off his hands. "We have to go," he said out loud.

He grabbed Squiggles by the arm and pulled him off Heat Vixen. Trent picked his laptop up off the bed and dragged the little hero out the door, trailing blood and slime into the sterile hall.

Slumping against the wall, Trent typed, *Get us there.*

The boy struggled to his feet, flinging blood and yellow gore from his hands. *They will pay for that.*

He led Trent down the white hallway.

After passing through two sets of thick metal doors that Squiggles opened with a wave of his hand, they found the machine powering the shield. A vast stack of generators and servers were imbedded in the black rock of the deep earth. They stood in a wide, dark cave with a slick, seamless floor.

The moment the super boy saw the shield's power source, he understood how to turn it off. But before he could do that, there were safeguards to bypass.

Two cyber-troopers came to life when Trent and Squiggles entered the cavernous power room. The robots charged their weapons—one's gun-hand glowed bright blue—and they sprang toward the intruders.

Trent screamed, pulling at Squiggles as he ran toward the rocky wall of the cave.

Squiggles shook him off. He faced the charging cyber-troopers.

There was a whining sound of weaponry, and a bright blue flash.

Rolling across the floor, hugging his laptop tight, Trent saw Squiggles raise his hand and make a twisting motion with it. The cyber-trooper with the glowing gun swung his weapon at the other robot as he fired it. The second cyber-trooper froze in mid-step. Electricity swarmed over its metallic body. It shook and shimmied and sparks popped from its faceplate. It fell over, clattering in a heap.

The remaining cyber-trooper raised its glowing gun to its head and pulled the trigger. The robot soldier shook with blue fire, and crashed down in front of Squiggles. Sparks and blood splashed off the smooth black floor.

"Holy shit!" Trent yelled.

In a blink, the power generator's huge hum fell silent.

Trent typed, *Is that it?*

Squiggles nodded.

He looked at the cyber-troopers. *Then let's get out of here.*

They ran back the way they came, Trent pulling the boy past the door marked with blood.

He wasn't thinking when he burst through the door and found that the guards had returned to their post. Trent burst through the door, saw the guards, screamed, and smacked into the wall. He held onto the laptop as he rebounded and hit the floor.

Squiggles waved his hand toward the guards. They fell to their knees in agony, screaming against the high-pitched tone from their earpieces. Blood poured from their noses and they gagged and sputtered, kicking in circles on the floor. The boy gathered his friend and they ran out of the underground.

Trent and Squiggles burst from the building into the open. The shield was down.

Soldiers ran toward the perimeter of the base, firing their guns wildly. Super people came tearing through the trees into the open fields of the base. Fire balls and lightning flew. Their forces were arriving.

Trent held the boy's hand and ran. Bullets ripped the ground.

An explosion blasted the air behind them, and they pitched forward as the shockwave hit. Squiggles helped Trent to his feet in time for him to see the squad of soldiers running at them.

Trent put his hand in the air, snuggling the laptop to his side.

A scorpion robot charged into the onrushing soldiers— its treads tearing apart their legs and feet, and its long metal arms whipping their bodies into chunks of meat.

Trent looked to Squiggles. The boy nodded feverishly. He took Trent's hand and pulled him onboard the gory scorpion.

A meteor of ice whistled in, smashing half of a building to rubble. It rolled across the field, crushing soldiers and pinning a cyber-trooper against another building. Trent saw a row of men evaporate in a gush of blood and a towering villain with a tube-shaped arm tromp through the space they'd occupied.

Squiggles drove them out of there and back up to the command post, weaving through the spreading fight.

Trent rolled off the scorpion-bot. Jen ran to him.

Martin stopped recording the battle and joined them. "Holy fuck, you did it!"

Trent nodded, gasping and guzzling the water that Jen provided. He dumped some on his head and pointed at Squiggles. "He did it."

The boy smiled.

Madame Manifestor and Big Burner were in the command bunker. They greeted Trent and Squiggles and went back to watching the battle. Couriers ran to and from them, passing information at super speed to the troop leaders below.

Jen said, "As soon as the shield dropped, they rushed it." She helped Trent up and led him to the vantage.

Soldiers poured from the buildings that weren't destroyed.

"Where are they all coming from?" Martin asked.

"Underground," Trent said. "The place is huge. Levels and levels. It's hard to say what's down there." He looked through the binoculars Jen handed him.

The super people near the buildings were taking damage. Soldiers outnumbered them, and there were cyber-troopers among them, blasting plasma and fire. The second wave of super people was tearing through the outer perimeter of soldiers, but more and more reinforced them.

"We're going down there," Trent said. He typed, *Do you think you can control those machines?*

Of course!

Trent jumped on the scorpion.

"Fucking crazy-ass," Martin said.

"Record this!" Trent yelled as Squiggles jumped on and the scorpion took off.

"Be careful!" Jen yelled.

They drove straight into the smoke and fighting.

Trent typed madly as they bumped through the battle on their hijacked robo-vehicle. *If you ca control lot of cynbr-soldiears, we can winnow!*

I have one now.

The scorpion skidded to a stop.

Squiggles jumped off it, his arms waving like a conductor. The battle raged around them.

A large, black and red villain with a red laser-arm like a glowing sword ran hacking soldiers in half and cauterizing them as they fell. Three military men took cover in the rubble of a ruined building, taking shots at whoever came past. One had a rocket launcher aimed at the demonlike laser swordsman.

A pink super woman jumped out from behind the building—Fuzzy Nightmare. Her suit covered her head to toe, with varying shades of pink outlining her breasts and pubic area. She was super sexy, even in the middle of the fight.

Like Death Killer, only her mouth and chin were suitless flesh. She smiled and giggled, pointing her hands at the soldiers like guns. Pink bolts of energy burst from her fingers. A blast of light hit one of the soldiers, turning him into a pink bunny. The next soldier saw what happened and tried to run, but was also turned into a bunny. The rocket launcher guy managed to get off his shot just as a pink burst hit him.

The rocket screamed through the air at the tall demon villain, but he was too busy slicing a soldier to burning bits. Fuzzy Nightmare shot a pink energy blast at the traveling rocket. Just as the villain turned around, a pink bunny slammed into his chest and he grabbed it out of reflex. When he looked down at what he'd caught, his big fluffy speech bubble read, *Awwwww.*

Five cyber-troopers crashed through the nearest building, stomping soldiers into squished bits, and shooting plasma at the other cyber-troopers in the battle.

Trent typed, *All yours?*

The boy nodded. *I can control five at once.* He sent them across to the other side of the clearing where other cyber-troopers fired on a knot of super people.

Trent gave Squiggles a thumbs-up.

Bullets ripped into the scorpion, ricocheting and spattering Trent with hot metal.

Lieutenant Rockwood stood with a rifle, aiming it straight at Trent. He yelled, "Fucking capeback lover! Get some!" He failed to see the large round villain who walked up behind him.

The Detonator crept up behind the lieutenant and displayed his ability.

The super man blew himself up in an impressive fireball and concussion—spraying the Lieutenant into warm pieces of bloody soldier that showered the grass. Rockwood's boots swayed and toppled where he'd stood. The Detonator reappeared in a swirl of colorful flesh-mist.

"Fuck you," Trent said. He fell to his knees.

A helicopter whumped overhead. Super people fell to its heavy guns. Rockets flared, and explosions rocked the main assault wave. Colorful, scorched body parts fell from the blurry sky.

The chopper suddenly pitched and with a short-lived wail, dumped itself into the ground, flattening three soldiers and dicing a few more to slaw with its rotors. The helicopter whipped itself into wreckage and caught fire. Men dragged themselves away, burning and screaming.

Trent got up and looked to Squiggles. The boy gave him a thumbs-up.

Super people advanced on the base. Soldiers were dying and retreating all around them.

Trent led Squiggles toward the rear of the battle. The boy kept control of the cyber-soldiers, and sent them cleaning up the stronger pockets of soldiers.

They made it to relative safety. At least to a place where they could rest while the heroes and villains pushed forward, surrounding the base. Trent climbed upon a captured guard platform and surveyed the battle.

Super people were closing in. Not many soldiers were left alive to resist, and those that lived were on the retreat.

Trent watched Big Burner lead a large force forward through the base in an arrow-shaped formation. They approached the shed that led to the underground part of the base. Just as they neared the little metal shack, the ground exploded underneath them.

The super people were thrown back or swallowed by the boiling earth as a wide hole opened in the field and a swarm of cyber-troopers poured into the sky like a plague of giant metal locusts. Hundreds upon hundreds of them.

The cyber-troopers tore from the hole in the field, blazing into the air. Shining metal glinted in the sun. A steady stream of terrible weapons snaked upward, expanding and opening into a raining funnel of fury directed back down at the ground.

"Fuck," Trent said.

159

The staggered super people gaped at the number of the cyber-troopers pouring from the earth. Fearsome weapons multiplied by the thousands turned downward, and the robot warriors attacked as a furious hive. The super people hesitated, gathering themselves, then took to the air to engage the enemy.

Squiggles clenched his eyes closed tight, and sent his five cyber-soldiers into the fight.

Chapter Thirty-Five

Trent tucked the laptop under his arm, grabbed Squiggles by the arm, and ran for the ridge. He hoped that there was still a reserve of super people on the other side of it. He searched the rock outcroppings and hasty log bunkers for Jen and Martin as he scrambled up the hill, dragging Squiggles along.

The top of the ridge exploded in fire.

Rocks, trees, dirt, and flame washed over the side of the hill. Trent jumped behind a boulder and pulled Squiggles close. Dirt rained down on them with burning bits of leaves, tree pieces, and body parts. Rocks and tree trunks rolled down into the jungle. The blast reverberated, shaking the ground.

A few super people tried to fly away from whatever hit them, but they flipped through the air to land dead in trees or crash to the ground with the rest of the debris. A wall of cyber-troopers rose over the ridge, weapons blasting at the surviving super people.

A super hero ran from the rubble spitting rocks at the cyber-troopers.

Squiggles looked up at Trent as the dust whirled. He pointed toward the base.

Trent turned to where the boy pointed. It seemed the only place left with any sort of protection. He and Squiggles ran back to the skirmish below. He assumed Jen and Martin were dead.

A tight line of super people defended against a growing barrage of cyber-troopers.

Trent saw Fuzzy Nightmare dangling from a cyber-soldier's claw. She shot pink bolts at it but it twisted her around each time, aiming her like a gun. The Detonator was hit, and turned into a fat pink bunny that promptly exploded. The pink villain finally hit the cyber-trooper, and she fell onto its little bunny body, crushing it. But a cyber-foot from the sky crashed down on her. Trent saw a pink flash.

Cyber-troopers advanced—plasma flying, ice freezing, terrible mechanized feet stomping. Heroes and villains fell from the sky

Squiggles tapped the laptop, settling down behind a mass of uprooted trees. Trent opened it.

I have control of thirty cyber-troopers. But there are nine hundred and eighty-nine active at this moment. I'm gaining more and more control, and I'm taking them out as well, but they are overwhelming me. And our forces. I have freed many of the fliers who were first incapacitated. They've rejoined the battle. There is a line of fighting just a hundred yards to our east where your friends are. We should go there.

Trent nodded. He heard a whirring sound and felt something pass by his midsection. It slammed into the little hero. Squiggles slumped forward unconscious with a growing knot on his bleeding head. A rock lay in his lap.

"Squiggles!" Trent shook him gently. The boy was limp. Trent picked him up and ran into the jungle. He struggled through the dense growth, carrying unconscious Squiggles.

Trent ran east, with explosions and fire tearing through the trees. He ran from the pounding feet of approaching cyber-troopers and straight into Martin and Jen hiding in a trench. Martin was still filming. He had the camera pointed at the sky.

Trent jumped into the trench, collapsing with Squiggles on top of him.

Jen yelled, "Oh no! What happened?"

"He was hit by a rock."

"Is he dead?"

Trent was crying. He shook his head. "I don't know."

Fire roared above them, sucking the oxygen out of the hole. Martin tumbled against the far wall of the trench. Most of his hair was kinky-black singed. The flames rolled over them, and hot air choked them. They gasped for breath as super body parts fell around them.

"I knew it was a bad idea to go up against these guys!" Martin yelled, one hand patting at his smoking head and the other pointing the camera out of the trench at the action.

"He's alive," Jen said, feeling the boy's pulse.

Trent nodded dumbly. He doubted that it mattered if Squiggles was alive. Without him controlling the cyber-troopers, they didn't have a chance.

On Shark Tooth Mountain, above the battle, but not removed from it, Death Killer sat looking down. He watched the cyber-troopers gathering in a thick cloud over the base—a gleaming stream of giant killer bees.

The villain stretched a torn white balloon over his knee so that he could read what was written on it—the last thing Trent had said.

Then do it for her.

He wanted to tear the balloon to bits. Then he thought about it.

Death Killer launched himself into the air. In the six seconds it took to arrive at the battle, he wondered if Trent was still alive. And if Maddie still loved him.

Small groups of super people held-off growing numbers of cyber-troopers in the air and amid the trees.

"Where is Madame Manifestor?" Trent yelled.

Something exploded beside them, sending dirt showering down.

Martin shrugged.

Jen said, "She was at the command post with Big Burner when it went up. We haven't seen them since." She picked dirt out of her ear.

Trent poked his head up and saw three heroes and a villain fighting five of the metal soldiers, each of them falling to the cyber-troopers. A super woman with blue hair and a red suit with a white butterfly chest emblem flew out from between two cyber-troopers that rammed into each other. Another robot shot a thick red laser from the back of its head while it grappled with a super man who puffed up into a spiny brown ball. The beam struck the heroine in the face, burning through it and exploding her skull.

The puffy brown villain screamed as the cyber-trooper pulled his stubby arms from his inflated body. A blast of ice froze the cyber-trooper's arms before it could do more, but it also hit the puffy villain, who cracked and burst.

Trent ducked as pieces of the body rained down.

Jen yelled, "We're gonna fuckin' diiiiiiiiie!"

Injured heroes and villains fell into the trench at an enormous rate. Explosions and bursts of super materials flew over their heads. Blood, and gore, and smoke and fire overwhelmed their senses. The sound of mechanized men stomping the jungle to squirming, burning bits of battle-jetsam rose above the din.

And then there was something new. It was the sound of the cyber-troopers stopping their advance and retreating. A thudding, whirring, running-away sound. Trent dared a glance over the edge of the trench.

The shattered jungle smoked in front of him. Through the falling debris and sunlit smoke, Trent could see outlines of weary villains and staggering heroes. They watched their foe turn and run. Trent looked to see if Squiggles was awake and controlling them. Sadly, he was not.

Trent jumped out of the hole and followed the curious super people from the battle site to see what had drawn away the cyber soldiers.

Martin yelled from behind him, "Look!"

A wide line of cyber-troopers whistled through the air like the barbed tail of a fighting kite, or an angry swarm of cartoon bees.

Death Killer swooped over the top of the smoldering jungle canopy and floated fifty feet above the trees, meeting the rocketing robots with punches, kicks, fire, plasma, ice, and mental energy. He grappled, shot them with laser eyes, crushed them, and used them as bowling balls and baseball bats. He burned them, tore off their heads, drove them into the ground, and blew them apart.

Other super people joined him in the sky. Trent was pretty sure he saw Madame Manifestor rushing to the villain's side.

"Death Killer!" Trent yelled.

Martin whooped.

Trent watched his friend leading the super people toward victory. Death Killer punched back a line of cyber-troopers toward the base as more poured from the wide hole in the ground. Other heroes gained ground. New sounds of battle erupted in front of the students.

The able super people near the trench rushed toward the base, leaping over burning stumps and flashing through the shadows, smoke, and debris. Gunfire came in bursts throughout the jungle.

"Jen, stay with Squiggles! I have to see what happens!" Trent ran off toward the base.

Martin looked at Jen.

"Go film it," she said.

A thousand cyber-troopers swarmed the sky. Death Killer held his place in the air. He was beating them back as they attacked. No more came from the base. Very few were on the ground. Super people fell from the sky or were blown to bits all around Death Killer as he raged.

Trent stood at the edge of the trees, watching the villain save the day. It was clear that Madame Manifestor fought beside him. Her white hair and red suit shone in the sun.

The ground fighting had moved to the flattened base. Super people were taking out the last of the soldiers. Not much but colorful suits flashed through the grass and building ruins.

Suddenly something new flew from the center of the base.

A massive cyber-trooper, easily the size of three, came blasting out of the hole in the ground. It spun through the air and straight into the swarming mass of cyber-soldiers.

Death Killer fought the cyber-troopers that came for him, but kept an eye on the metallic cloud in the distance. Something was happening within that silver swarm.

Trent saw it, too.

That bigger cyber-trooper was gathering the others. The cyber-soldiers attached themselves together. A longer and thicker bunch of them gathered just above the ground.

Death Killer was kept busy with a steady stream to fight. It seemed as if all the other flying super people were suddenly down. Trent couldn't even see Madame Manifestor. The mass of robots swelled.

Soon there was a solid cube of mashed-together cyber-soldiers. It spun slowly in the air, shining and glinting. The cube grew two tails that reached toward the ground. More and more cyber-troopers gathered, joining the mass—clinking and clattering into a giant, solid thing. The tails became legs that stretched to the ground.

Those legs started stomping across the jungle, crushing trees and leaving deep footprints shaped like fifty cyber-troopers on their metallic backs. It grew two tentacle arms that whipped toward the super villain in the sky. Trent stood gaping up at a seventy-five-foot tall cyber-trooper constructed of a thousand smaller ones.

The giant cyber-soldier rampaged toward Death Killer. It shot a laser beam as wide as a bus at the super man. Trent heard sizzling over the cracking of trees and the tromping of giant robot feet as Death Killer dodged it.

The cyber-giant's head was the larger cyber-trooper. Inside it was Colonel Shank. Trent could see him fairly clearly as the huge thing stomped past. He worked over-sized joysticks, driving the giant robot and, swinging its mountainous fists at the tiny super villain in the sky. The colonel yelled into a microphone, and his shrill military voice tore across the air. "I'm gonna fuck you up, capeback!"

Trent said quietly, "He can't understand you, asshole."

But even if he couldn't, Death Killer understood the situation. With a gleeful smile, he grew.

In less than a second, a one hundred-foot-tall super villain stood snarling at the giant robot. His massive black claws dug into the earth. He opened his big, pointy mouth and roared. Flames shot out from between his double rows of mountain-peak teeth.

Death Killer's eyes were two mean suns shining through his giant black mask. Muscles rippled over his body like continents rearranging themselves. Blue plasma coursed over his huge hands. Volcanoes of fire burst from the horns on his head. Trent remembered his first up-close encounter with the villain.

A tree creaked and fell in front of Trent. It snapped him back to his own immediate situation. He was in the burning jungle. There was still fighting going on around him. A scorpion vehicle lie on its back just ahead—its tracks spinning furiously, catching bits of debris and sling-shooting it into the trees.

At the base, super people swarmed down holes to ferret-out whoever and whatever was left underground. Gunfire peppered the air on the far side of the clearing. Trent saw Big Burner and Madame Manifestor leading a group down the big cyber-trooper hole. He was happy they were alive.

Ash fell on him, and Trent ran into the clearing, away from giant stomping feet. He dove behind a mound of scorched cinderblocks. That's when he realized that Martin was with him.

"Holy shit! I didn't know you were here!" Trent yelled, smiling and patting the frat boy's shoulder.

"Look at that shit!" Martin yelled, filming the fight.

The giant cyber-trooper drove into the villain's body, rushing through a wall of flame. It wrapped its snaking appendages around Death Killer, pinning the villain's arms to his sides. The robot tried to drag him down.

Death Killer flexed his arms and the robot's flung wide. The super villain grabbed hold of the flopping robot arms and pulled them off the giant body. He crumpled the arms together, and tossed the ragged ball of cyber-garbage into the ocean while the colonel shrieked into the microphone and pulled back on his joysticks.

The cyber-giant staggered backward. It stomped across the base, flattening two super people and tripping in a scorpion hole. The huge robot caught its balance and transformed as Death Killer ran toward it. Shank pushed buttons and stared out the wide, clear faceplate of his large cyber-trooper command pod-thing.

The robot shrank, shifting cyber-troopers from its legs in a grinding conveyor belt across its boxy torso, and sprouted new arms just as Death Killer swung a massive fist at its Colonel-filled head. The giant cyber-soldier managed to block the blow, but its new arm was crushed in the process, and cyber-troopers flew apart—scattering to fall across the island.

Its other arm was melted to slag as Colonel Shank raised it just in time to save himself from Death Killer's laser eyes. The giant cyber-trooper staggered backward.

The ruined arm detached itself at the shoulder and slammed to the ground near Trent. A few living cyber-troopers broke off from their fused, smoldering brethren, and jumped down holes into the underground.

The giant villain snatched the fleeing robot by its roiling midsection as the metal monster tried to rearrange itself again into a smaller, more capable machine. As cyber-troopers poured outward in snaky new arms, Death Killer drove his claws into the giant robot's chest and pulled it apart, ripping the smaller cyber-troopers to whirring, screeching bits, smashing them and kicking at the metal monster's crumbling legs.

Death Killer mashed little robots in his giant plasmatic hands. They popped like beer cans in a bonfire. He swept lasers and fire into the fleeing cyber-troopers and stomped the scrambling pieces of the mega-bot. They shot tiny bolts of lasers, ice, and fire at him. He kicked, burned, and squished most to death. A few flew off, or went down the holes. Super people scrambled to round them up.

Trent and Martin dodged toppling cinderblocks and chunks of falling metal as the towering villain tore the cyber-giant apart. Trent couldn't believe Martin's filming tenacity. The frat boy had been taping everything since the battle began. He was a mud and ash-smeared, bloody wreck of sweat and grime, and he was whooping with glee as he captured the military's last moments.

Death Killer held the giant robot's head in his massive claws.

A huge, jagged speech bubble shot from the villain's mouth. *THE END!* It burst loudly across the faceplate of Shank's vehicle.

Death Killer stared into the cockpit while the colonel pushed buttons that shot useless projectiles at the giant. The big villain gnashed his terrible teeth at the tiny unmasked thing inside its metal trap. Then he smashed it until blood squirted between his claws. He let it fall to the ground.

The super man stomped a fleeing pack of cyber-soldiers, grinding them to gritty junk.

He shrunk himself back to normal size and floated to the ground at the edge of the clearing.

Trent and Martin ran to join him.

There were muffled sounds of fighting coming from the holes in the ground, and a flash from the big one. Trent was confident that the super people were winning the fight down there. Martin swung the camera across the field as they ran, capturing the end of the battle as best he could.

Death Killer saw them coming.

He greeted Trent with a deep happy smile, and a hug. He nodded to Martin over the student's shoulder.

Trent searched his shredded pockets for balloons and came up empty.

Martin handed him a handful. And a marker.

Thank you, Trent said to Death Killer.

The villain's bubbles were smooth and round. *Thank YOU, Trent. You saved the island.*

Shut up. You did.

The villain grinned. *I have to go find Maddie—Madame Manifestor.*

Go. Trent smiled.

Death Killer nodded, jumped into the air, and flew into the big hole.

Trent heard the sound of a motor off to his left. He tapped Martin on the shoulder. "Hear that?"

They ran through the bushes to the beach.

Martin had the camera rolling. "Look!" he shouted, pointing.

Out on the ocean, a boatload of soldiers attempted their escape. A military boat, armored and loaded with guns, bounced out across the surf.

"We need to get someone!" Trent yelled.

"Wait," said Martin. "Look over there."

Whalemancer's head stuck out above the choppy waves. Circles of psychic energy poured from his head.

A young white whale broke the surface of the water a hundred yards from the fleeing craft. It sped toward the soldiers on collision-course. The gunner noticed the whale just before they hit each other. He opened fire, pelting the whale with fifty-caliber bullets. Red geysers shot from the whale's big white back as it raised its head and rammed the charging boat.

The boat exploded. Screaming men hit the water dead or dying. Frothing whale blood, brains, and bone filled the water as the beast rolled and spasmed, its tail lifting out of the waves and smacking down on a swimming soldier. Whalemancer swam a happy circle through flotsam, fuel and blood, picking off survivors one-by-one by twisting their necks with his big tentacle arms.

"Got enough footage of *that*?" Trent asked.

"Definitely. Let's get out of here."

They stumbled back toward the base. Super people emerged from the underground base. Madame Manifestor flew out with Death Killer. Big Burner followed them closely. When Death Killer saw the students, he swooped down to meet them. A crowd pressed around the villain, reaching out to thank him. He let them.

Jen came through a cloud of smoke with a group of injured super people at the opposite edge of the clearing. Squiggles walked beside her, holding her hand. He had the laptop tucked under his other arm. Trent ran to hug the little guy.

A few days later, after most of the fires were extinguished, the wounded tended to, and temporary housing arranged, Trent and the rest of the students gathered with the super people.

Squiggles sat beside Trent. He said, *Death Killer and Madame Manifestor leading us together. That feels good. I'm happy Big Burner stepped down gracefully.*

Trent looked at the boy, and then to the super people standing in front of them. He typed, *I agree.*

Death Killer stood before a semi-circle of seated super people at Villain Village. He spoke to them with smooth, round bubbles about his ideas for combining the tribes. Madame Manifestor stood beside him, with her arm wrapped around the villain's waist. She smiled up at him now and then.

Trent looked at the colorful scene in front of him. All the super people of the island together made a brilliant palette. He burned the image into his memory since his notebook was tucked in his pack.

Jen said, "It's pretty cool that Squiggles was able to transmit the video and computer data to all the world's news services simultaneously." She squeezed the kid's shoulder.

"Yeah, he's pretty amazing," Trent said. He typed to him what Jen said.

Squiggles smiled at her.

"I think it's cool, too," said Martin. He leaned into the bosom of the super woman at his side. "I'll be a famous documentary cinematographer."

Jen laughed. "And I'll be an investigative reporter."

Trent made eye contact with Death Killer over the heads of the gathered islanders. The super man smiled at him and nodded. His eyes flared, and he pulled Madame Manifestor close.

Epilogue

After every news agency on the planet received the uplink from Squiggles and aired the story, the cyber-trooper program was immediately shut down. The public outcry forced changes in the operations of militaries across the world.

It also led to changes on the Island of the Super People. Now that the rest of the world was aware of their existence, super people were suddenly a part of the global network. And it was not long before some of them left the island and were integrated into the rest of society—taking up lives befitting super folk in metropolises, small burgs, and wherever they felt they were wanted, needed, or comfortable.

Many of them found satisfaction among the unmasked. A few of them left and returned to the island to live their simpler lives. Some never ventured from their home. At least one of them got stuck doing a fairly miserable job out in the world—but it really was his fault.

All in all, things became a little bit better everywhere.

Death Killer and Madame Manifestor had a lavish wedding befitting the leaders of the Island of the Super People.

The super man's horns were polished and his eyes glowed softly beneath his scarred mask. Madame Manifestor was dazzling and as beautiful as ever. She floated in with a trail of webbing from her spinnerets.

Super people lit the sky with their powers, made sweet music, and many happy speech bubbles expanded and popped at the culmination of the couple's vows. Big Burner gave a tearful, touching speech that had everyone sobbing joyfully in the end.

The super couple ruled the island for many years from their gleaming fortress on Shark Tooth Mountain. They had several children born with all sorts of colored suits. Their kids grew up on a different island than their parents had, and made many decisions for themselves about who they would be on it.

Death Killer was never again considered a villain. He became the most loved super person on the planet when he saved the Earth from a collision with a planet-cracking comet. And then later when he stopped Super Evil, a pretty terrible villain, from turning every ounce of water in the world into poison.

Trent's field notes from his time spent on the island were published as a book. It was an instant bestseller and he gained worldwide recognition for his diplomatic efforts. Trent was named the UN Ambassador to the Island. He met Professor Topper's daughter, Mechele, at a ceremony held in her father's honor. Mechele painted and liked photographing flowers. It didn't take long for them to fall in love.

As the UN Ambassador, Trent lived in a swank cottage near the dock, just up the beach from where he'd first seen Whalemancer beach the feast for the Crossover Ceremony. He and Mechele spent a good deal of time there, hanging out with super friends and watching the sun set.

The couple spent many days on Shark Tooth Mountain as well, with Trent's best friend DK, and Maddie. When the super man wasn't off saving the planet, Trent and Death Killer collaborated on art pieces that ended up in galleries across the world.

Martin became a famous documentary cinematographer. His footage of the battle for the island was made into a six-hour film and also used for several documentaries. It was some of the most viewed footage in all of history. Later, he filmed an exposé on one of his super girlfriends—Damselfly—as she made her bid for Miss Universe. He was constantly being asked for interviews, which he sometimes gave by satellite uplink from his beachside bungalow that he'd named, The Luscious Lair. He lived happily with six super women.

Martin spent most of his time at home on the island, now and then hanging out with Trent and Death Killer, fishing or playing disc golf.

Jen went back to school and finished her degree in anthropology. She studied super people in urban settings and her notes were published as a book and made into a movie and sit-com. Her work also spawned a short-lived reality show called, *The Super World*, which put a super person into an apartment with six strangers to see what would happen when he or she stopped being nice, and kept being super.

One day on the beach in St. Lucia, Jen overheard a conversation about an island north of Ireland where real leprechauns lived—an enchanted, elf-like people from the center of the Earth with nearly translucent skin and control over the elements.

Jen took the next ship headed north. The last anyone heard from her was four months later, when she called Trent from Edinburgh to tell him that a super person friend of hers had found the Island of the Leprechauns for her, and that she'd be away for a while.

Whalemancer made some bad decisions after the battle for the island. He fell-in with pirates who talked him into helping them hunt whales. It didn't take much to persuade the super man—he hated whales.

He was very bitter about them being the only creatures in the sea that he could communicate with and control. And they were such assholes to him. They always tried to talk him out of beaching them by using some New Age love and light seahorseshit, or logic. *Oh, don't kill me*, they would say telepathically, *I'm a higher life form, blah blah blah.* So he teamed up with the pirates, and any other whaling vessels he could find after that.

Within two years he had personally caused the death of all but one whale in the world. A single whale survived out of the entire whale population on Earth. And it lived at Sea World.

Whalemancer was apprehended by Death Killer and the UN. They made him pay reparations for the decimation of an entire species. He was forced to spend the rest of his days at Sea World, tending to the last whale's every need. He became its handler, nursemaid, and nanny. He fed the whale. He cleaned the huge whale poop from its tank. He dealt with the public and put on shows. Whalemancer was not very happy. Not ever.

Squiggles moved to Japan. He was hired by Shimushitzu Incorporated a week after the island war went public. The super boy started out creating electronic gadgets and gear. He produced his video game—*Fern Fight!*

It wasn't long until Squiggles owned a company of his own. Squiggles Technologies soon demolished the competition. Amazing technology began to appear in the world—starting with personal translators that allowed anyone to speak Super-Person.

But that was only the beginning. Squiggles changed the world dramatically with his electro-powers and inventions. Free energy for everyone was a big deal. So were teleportation, ram-jets, and the quantum reticulator. He built his own floating island with a fortress/theme park, where he lived like a techno-king.

Squiggles stepped through his teleporter to visit the Island of the Super People at least twice a month. He went fishing with the boys now and then, or sat and watched Trent and Death Killer sculpt or paint. He spent good times in his fort in the jungle—inviting all of his friends to interactive, found-art light and sound shows.

He was nearly always happy.

KEVIN SHAMEL is the author of, *Rotten Little Animals*, and soon to be released, *Porn Land*. He has super freckle power and is a perv for Poison Ivy.

Bizarro books

CATALOG   SPRING 2011

Bizarro Books publishes under the following imprints:

www.rawdogscreamingpress.com

www.eraserheadpress.com

www.afterbirthbooks.com

www.swallowdownpress.com

For all your Bizarro needs visit:

WWW.BIZARROCENTRAL.COM

Introduce yourselves to the bizarro fiction genre and all of its authors with the Bizarro Starter Kit series. Each volume features short novels and short stories by ten of the leading bizarro authors, designed to give you a perfect sampling of the genre for only $10.

BB-0X1
"The Bizarro Starter Kit" (Orange)

Featuring D. Harlan Wilson, Carlton Mellick III, Jeremy Robert Johnson, Kevin L Donihe, Gina Ranalli, Andre Duza, Vincent W. Sakowski, Steve Beard, John Edward Lawson, and Bruce Taylor.
236 pages $10

BB-0X2
"The Bizarro Starter Kit" (Blue)

Featuring Ray Fracalossy, Jeremy C. Shipp, Jordan Krall, Mykle Hansen, Andersen Prunty, Eckhard Gerdes, Bradley Sands, Steve Aylett, Christian TeBordo, and Tony Rauch. **244 pages $10**

BB-0X2
"The Bizarro Starter Kit" (Purple)

Featuring Russell Edson, Athena Villaverde, David Agranoff, Matthew Revert, Andrew Goldfarb, Jeff Burk, Garrett Cook, Kris Saknussemm, Cody Goodfellow, and Cameron Pierce **264 pages $10**

BB-001"**The Kafka Effekt**" **D. Harlan Wilson** - A collection of forty-four irreal short stories loosely written in the vein of Franz Kafka, with more than a pinch of William S. Burroughs sprinkled on top. **211 pages $14**

BB-002 "**Satan Burger**" **Carlton Mellick III** - The cult novel that put Carlton Mellick III on the map ... Six punks get jobs at a fast food restaurant owned by the devil in a city violently overpopulated by surreal alien cultures. **236 pages $14**

BB-003 "**Some Things Are Better Left Unplugged**" **Vincent Sakowski** - Join The Man and his Nemesis, the obese tabby, for a nightmare roller coaster ride into this postmodern fantasy. **152 pages $10**

BB-004 "**Shall We Gather At the Garden?**" **Kevin L Donihe** - Donihe's Debut novel. Midgets take over the world, The Church of Lionel Richie vs. The Church of the Byrds, plant porn and more! **244 pages $14**

BB-005 "**Razor Wire Pubic Hair**" **Carlton Mellick III** - A genderless humandildo is purchased by a razor dominatrix and brought into her nightmarish world of bizarre sex and mutilation.   **176 pages $11**

BB-006 "**Stranger on the Loose**" **D. Harlan Wilson** - The fiction of Wilson's 2nd collection is planted in the soil of normalcy, but what grows out of that soil is a dark, witty, otherworldly jungle... **228 pages $14**

BB-007 "**The Baby Jesus Butt Plug**" **Carlton Mellick III** - Using clones of the Baby Jesus for anal sex will be the hip sex fetish of the future. **92 pages $10**

BB-008 "**Fishyfleshed**" **Carlton Mellick III** - The world of the past is an illogical flatland lacking in dimension and color, a sick-scape of crispy squid people wandering the desert for no apparent reason. **260 pages $14**

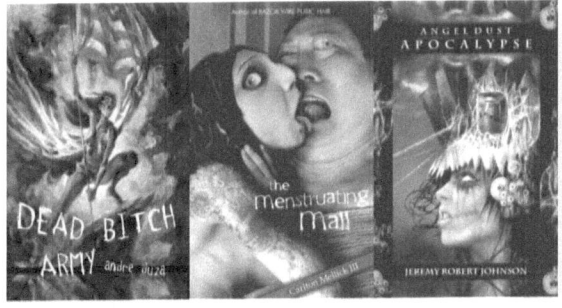

BB-009 "Dead Bitch Army" Andre Duza - Step into a world filled with racist teenagers, cannibals, 100 warped Uncle Sams, automobiles with razor-sharp teeth, living graffiti, and a pissed-off zombie bitch out for revenge. **344 pages $16**

BB-010 "The Menstruating Mall" Carlton Mellick III - "The Breakfast Club meets Chopping Mall as directed by David Lynch." - Brian Keene **212 pages $12**

BB-011 "Angel Dust Apocalypse" Jeremy Robert Johnson - Meth-heads, man-made monsters, and murderous Neo-Nazis. "Seriously amazing short stories..." - Chuck Palahniuk, author of Fight Club **184 pages $11**

BB-012 "Ocean of Lard" Kevin L Donihe / Carlton Mellick III - A parody of those old Choose Your Own Adventure kid's books about some very odd pirates sailing on a sea made of animal fat. **176 pages $12**

BB-015 "Foop!" Chris Genoa - Strange happenings are going on at Dactyl, Inc, the world's first and only time travel tourism company.
"A surreal pie in the face!" - Christopher Moore **300 pages $14**

BB-020 "Punk Land" Carlton Mellick III - In the punk version of Heaven, the anarchist utopia is threatened by corporate fascism and only Goblin, Mortician's sperm, and a blue-mohawked female assassin named Shark Girl can stop them. **284 pages $15**

BB-021 "Pseudo-City" D. Harlan Wilson - Pseudo-City exposes what waits in the bathroom stall, under the manhole cover and in the corporate boardroom, all in a way that can only be described as mind-bogglingly irreal. **220 pages $16**

BB-023 "Sex and Death In Television Town" Carlton Mellick III - In the old west, a gang of hermaphrodite gunslingers take refuge from a demon plague in Telos: a town where its citizens have televisions instead of heads. **184 pages $12**

BB-027 "Siren Promised" Jeremy Robert Johnson & Alan M Clark
- Nominated for the Bram Stoker Award. A potent mix of bad drugs, bad dreams, brutal bad guys, and surreal/incredible art by Alan M. Clark. **190 pages $13**

BB-030 "Grape City" Kevin L. Donihe - More Donihe-style comedic bizarro about a demon named Charles who is forced to work a minimum wage job on Earth after Hell goes out of business. **108 pages $10**

BB-031"Sea of the Patchwork Cats" Carlton Mellick III - A quiet dreamlike tale set in the ashes of the human race. For Mellick enthusiasts who also adore The Twilight Zone. **112 pages $10**

BB-032 "Extinction Journals" Jeremy Robert Johnson - An uncanny voyage across a newly nuclear America where one man must confront the problems associated with loneliness, insane dieties, radiation, love, and an ever-evolving cockroach suit with a mind of its own. **104 pages $10**

BB-034 "The Greatest Fucking Moment in Sports" Kevin L. Donihe
- In the tradition of the surreal anti-sitcom Get A Life comes a tale of triumph and agape love from the master of comedic bizarro. **108 pages $10**

BB-035 "The Troublesome Amputee" John Edward Lawson - Disturbing verse from a man who truly believes nothing is sacred and intends to prove it. **104 pages $9**

BB-037 "The Haunted Vagina" Carlton Mellick III - It's difficult to love a woman whose vagina is a gateway to the world of the dead. **132 pages $10**

BB-042 "Teeth and Tongue Landscape" Carlton Mellick III - On a planet made out of meat, a socially-obsessive monophobic man tries to find his place amongst the strange creatures and communities that he comes across. **110 pages $10**

BB-043 **"War Slut" Carlton Mellick III** - Part "1984," part "Waiting for Go-dot," and part action horror video game adaptation of John Carpenter's "The Thing." **116 pages $10**

BB-045 **"Dr. Identity" D. Harlan Wilson** - Follow the Dystopian Duo on a killing spree of epic proportions through the irreal postcapitalist city of Bliptown where time ticks sideways, artificial Bug-Eyed Monsters punish citizens for consumer-capitalist lethargy, and ultraviolence is as essential as a daily multivitamin. **208 pages $15**

BB-047 **"Sausagey Santa" Carlton Mellick III** - A bizarro Christmas tale featuring Santa as a piratey mutant with a body made of sausages. 124 pages $10

BB-048 **"Misadventures in a Thumbnail Universe" Vincent Sakowski** - Dive deep into the surreal and satirical realms of neo-classical Blender Fiction, filled with television shoes and flesh-filled skies. **120 pages $10**

BB-049 **"Vacation" Jeremy C. Shipp** - Blueblood Bernard Johnson leaved his boring life behind to go on The Vacation, a year-long corporate sponsored odyssey. But instead of seeing the world, Bernard is captured by terrorists, becomes a key figure in secret drug wars, and, worse, doesn't once miss his secure American Dream. **160 pages $14**

BB-053 **"Ballad of a Slow Poisoner" Andrew Goldfarb** Millford Mutter-wurst sat down on a Tuesday to take his afternoon tea, and made the unpleasant discovery that his elbows were becoming flatter. **128 pages $10**

BB-055 **"Help! A Bear is Eating Me" Mykle Hansen** - The bizarro, heart-warming, magical tale of poor planning, hubris and severe blood loss... **150 pages $11**

BB-056 **"Piecemeal June" Jordan Krall** - A man falls in love with a living sex doll, but with love comes danger when her creator comes after her with crab-squid assassins. **90 pages $9**

BB-058 "The Overwhelming Urge" Andersen Prunty - A collection of bizarro tales by Andersen Prunty. **150 pages $11**

BB-059 "Adolf in Wonderland" Carlton Mellick III - A dreamlike adventure that takes a young descendant of Adolf Hitler's design and sends him down the rabbit hole into a world of imperfection and disorder. **180 pages $11**

BB-061 "Ultra Fuckers" Carlton Mellick III - Absurdist suburban horror about a couple who enter an upper middle class gated community but can't find their way out. **108 pages $9**

BB-062 "House of Houses" Kevin L. Donihe - An odd man wants to marry his house. Unfortunately, all of the houses in the world collapse at the same time in the Great House Holocaust. Now he must travel to House Heaven to find his departed fiancee. **172 pages $11**

BB-064 "Squid Pulp Blues" Jordan Krall - In these three bizarro-noir novellas, the reader is thrown into a world of murderers, drugs made from squid parts, deformed gun-toting veterans, and a mischievous apocalyptic donkey. **204 pages $12**

BB-065 "Jack and Mr. Grin" Andersen Prunty - "When Mr. Grin calls you can hear a smile in his voice. Not a warm and friendly smile, but the kind that seizes your spine in fear. You don't need to pay your phone bill to hear it. That smile is in every line of Prunty's prose." - Tom Bradley. **208 pages $12**

BB-066 "Cybernetrix" Carlton Mellick III - What would you do if your normal everyday world was slowly mutating into the video game world from Tron? **212 pages $12**

BB-072 "Zerostrata" Andersen Prunty - Hansel Nothing lives in a tree house, suffers from memory loss, has a very eccentric family, and falls in love with a woman who runs naked through the woods every night. **144 pages $11**

BB-073 **"The Egg Man" Carlton Mellick III** - It is a world where humans reproduce like insects. Children are the property of corporations, and having an enormous ten-foot brain implanted into your skull is a grotesque sexual fetish. Mellick's industrial urban dystopia is one of his darkest and grittiest to date. **184 pages $11**

BB-074 **"Shark Hunting in Paradise Garden" Cameron Pierce** - A group of strange humanoid religious fanatics travel back in time to the Garden of Eden to discover it is invested with hundreds of giant flying maneating sharks. **150 pages $10**

BB-075 **"Apeshit" Carlton Mellick III** - Friday the 13th meets Visitor Q. Six hipster teens go to a cabin in the woods inhabited by a deformed killer. An incredibly fucked-up parody of B-horror movies with a bizarro slant. **192 pages $12**

BB-076 **"Fuckers of Everything on the Crazy Shitting Planet of the Vomit At mosphere" Mykle Hansen** - Three bizarro satires. Monster Cocks, Journey to the Center of Agnes Cuddlebottom, and Crazy Shitting Planet. **228 pages $12**

BB-077 **"The Kissing Bug" Daniel Scott Buck** - In the tradition of Roald Dahl, Tim Burton, and Edward Gorey, comes this bizarro anti-war children's story about a bohemian conenose kissing bug who falls in love with a human woman. **116 pages $10**

BB-078 **"MachoPoni" Lotus Rose** - It's My Little Pony... *Bizarro* style! A long time ago Poniworld was split in two. On one side of the Jagged Line is the Pastel King-dom, a magical land of music, parties, and positivity. On the other side of the Jagged Line is Dark Kingdom inhabited by an army of undead ponies. **148 pages $11**

BB-079 **"The Faggiest Vampire" Carlton Mellick III** - A Roald Dahl-esque children's story about two faggy vampires who partake in a mustache competition to find out which one is truly the faggiest. **104 pages $10**

BB-080 **"Sky Tongues" Gina Ranalli** - The autobiography of Sky Tongues, the biracial hermaphrodite actress with tongues for fingers. Follow her strange life story as she rises from freak to fame. **204 pages $12**

BB-081 **"Washer Mouth" Kevin L. Donihe** - A washing machine becomes human and pursues his dream of meeting his favorite soap opera star. **244 pages $11**

BB-082 **"Shatnerquake" Jeff Burk** - All of the characters ever played by William Shatner are suddenly sucked into our world. Their mission: hunt down and destroy the real William Shatner. **100 pages $10**

BB-083 **"The Cannibals of Candyland" Carlton Mellick III** - There exists a race of cannibals that are made of candy. They live in an underground world made out of candy. One man has dedicated his life to killing them all. **170 pages $11**

BB-084 **"Slub Glub in the Weird World of the Weeping Willows"** **Andrew Goldfarb** - The charming tale of a blue glob named Slub Glub who helps the weeping willows whose tears are flooding the earth. There are also hyenas, ghosts, and a voodoo priest **100 pages $10**

BB-085 **"Super Fetus" Adam Pepper** - Try to abort this fetus and he'll kick your ass! **104 pages $10**

BB-086 **"Fistful of Feet" Jordan Krall** - A bizarro tribute to spaghetti westerns, featuring Cthulhu-worshipping Indians, a woman with four feet, a crazed gunman who is obsessed with sucking on candy, Syphilis-ridden mutants, sexually transmitted tattoos, and a house devoted to the freakiest fetishes. **228 pages $12**

BB-087 **"Ass Goblins of Auschwitz" Cameron Pierce** - It's Monty Python meets Nazi exploitation in a surreal nightmare as can only be imagined by Bizarro author Cameron Pierce. **104 pages $10**

BB-088 **"Silent Weapons for Quiet Wars" Cody Goodfellow** - "This is high-end psychological surrealist horror meets bottom-feeding low-life crime in a techno-thrilling science fiction world full of Lovecraft and magic..." -John Skipp **212 pages $12**

BB-089 "Warrior Wolf Women of the Wasteland" Carlton Mellick III
Road Warrior Werewolves versus McDonaldland Mutants...post-apocalyptic fiction has
never been quite like this. **316 pages $13**

BB-090 "Cursed" Jeremy C Shipp - The story of a group of characters who
believe they are cursed and attempt to figure out who cursed them and why. A tale of
stylish absurdism and suspenseful horror. **218 pages $15**

BB-091 "Super Giant Monster Time" Jeff Burk - A tribute to choose your
own adventures and Godzilla movies. Will you escape the giant monsters that are rampaging
the fuck out of your city and shit? Or will you join the mob of alien-controlled punk rockers
causing chaos in the streets? What happens next depends on you. **188 pages $12**

BB-092 "Perfect Union" Cody Goodfellow - "Cronenberg's THE FLY on a
grand scale: human/insect gene-spliced body horror, where the human hive politics are as
shocking as the gore." -John Skipp. **272 pages $13**

BB-093 "Sunset with a Beard" Carlton Mellick III - 14 stories of surreal
science fiction. **200 pages $12**

BB-094 "My Fake War" Andersen Prunty - The absurd tale of an unlikely soldier
forced to fight a war that, quite possibly, does not exist. It's Rambo meets Waiting for Godot in
this subversive satire of American values and the scope of the human imagination. **128 pages $11**

BB-095"Lost in Cat Brain Land" Cameron Pierce - Sad stories from a surreal world. A fascist mustache, the ghost of Franz Kafka, a desert inside a dead cat. Primor-
dial entities mourn the death of their child. The desperate serve tea to mysterious creatures.
A hopeless romantic falls in love with a pterodactyl. And much more. **152 pages $11**

**BB-096 "The Kobold Wizard's Dildo of Enlightenment +2" Carlton
Mellick III** - A Dungeons and Dragons parody about a group of people who learn they
are only made up characters in an AD&D campaign and must find a way to resist their
nerdy teenaged players and retarded dungeon master in order to survive. **232 pages $12**

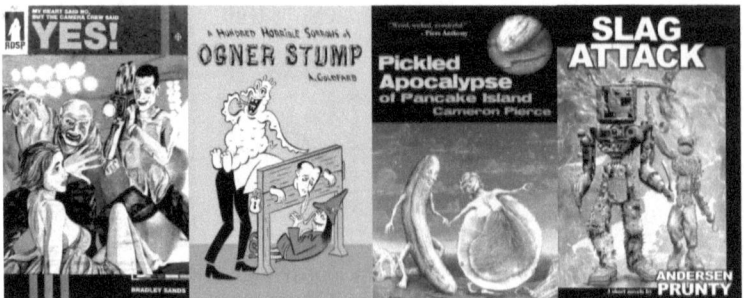

BB-097 **"My Heart Said No, but the Camera Crew Said Yes!"** Bradley
Sands - A collection of short stories that are crammed with the delightfully odd and the
scurrilously silly. **140 pages $13**

BB-098 **"A Hundred Horrible Sorrows of Ogner Stump"** Andrew
Goldfarb - Goldfarb's acclaimed comic series. A magical and weird journey into
the horrors of everyday life. **164 pages $11**

BB-099 **"Pickled Apocalypse of Pancake Island"** Cameron Pierce
A demented fairy tale about a pickle, a pancake, and the apocalypse. **102 pages $8**

BB-100 **"Slag Attack"** Andersen Prunty - Slag Attack features four visceral,
noir stories about the living, crawling apocalypse. A slag is what survivors are calling the
slug-like maggots raining from the sky, burrowing inside people, and hollowing out their
flesh and their sanity. **148 pages $11**

BB-101 **"Slaughterhouse High"** Robert Devereaux - A place where
schools are built with secret passageways, rebellious teens get zippers installed in their
mouths and genitals, and once a year, on that special night, one couple is slaughtered and
the bits of their bodies are kept as souvenirs. **304 pages $13**

BB-102 **"The Emerald Burrito of Oz"** John Skipp & Marc Levinthal
OZ IS REAL! Magic is real! The gate is really in Kansas! And America is finally allowing
Earth tourists to visit this weird-ass, mysterious land. But when Gene of Los Angeles heads off
for summer vacation in the Emerald City, little does he know that a war is brewing...a war that
could destroy both worlds. **280 pages $13**

BB-103 **"The Vegan Revolution... with Zombies"** David Agranoff
When there's no more meat in hell, the vegans will walk the earth. **160 pages $11**

BB-104 **"The Flappy Parts"** Kevin L Donihe - Poems about bunnies, LSD,
and police abuse. You know, things that matter. 132 **pages $11**

BB-105 **"Sorry I Ruined Your Orgy" Bradley Sands** - Bizarro humorist
Bradley Sands returns with one of the strangest, most hilarious collections of the year.
130 pages $11

BB-106 **"Mr. Magic Realism" Bruce Taylor** - Like Golden Age science fiction comics written by Freud, *Mr. Magic Realism* is a strange, insightful adventure that
spans the furthest reaches of the galaxy, exploring the hidden caverns in the hearts and
minds of men, women, aliens, and biomechanical cats. **152 pages $11**

BB-107 **"Zombies and Shit" Carlton Mellick III** - "Battle Royale" meets
"Return of the Living Dead." Mellick's bizarro tribute to the zombie genre. **308 pages $13**

BB-108 **"The Cannibal's Guide to Ethical Living" Mykle Hansen** -
Over a five star French meal of fine wine, organic vegetables and human flesh, a lunatic deliv-
ers a witty, chilling, disturbingly sane argument in favor of eating the rich.. **184 pages $11**

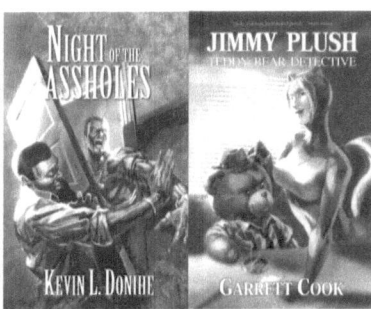

BB-109 **"Starfish Girl" Athena Villaverde** - In a post-apocalyptic underwater
dome society, a girl with a starfish growing from her head and an assassin with sea ane-
nome hair are on the run from a gang of mutant fish men. **160 pages $11**

BB-110 **"Lick Your Neighbor" Chris Genoa** - Mutant ninjas, a talking whale,
kung fu masters, maniacal pilgrims, and an alcoholic clown populate Chris Genoa's surreal,
darkly comical and unnerving reimagining of the first Thanksgiving. **303 pages $13**

BB-111 **"Night of the Assholes" Kevin L. Donihe** - A plague of assholes
is infecting the countryside. Normal everyday people are transforming into jerks, snobs,
dicks, and douchebags. And they all have only one purpose: to make your life a living hell..
192 pages $11

BB-112 **"Jimmy Plush, Teddy Bear Detective" Garrett Cook** - Hard-
boiled cases of a private detective trapped within a teddy bear body. **180 pages $11**